THE REINS
OF DANGER

THE HEATHER REED MYSTERY SERIES

THE REINS
OF DANGER

REBECCA PRICE JANNEY

WORD PUBLISHING

Dallas•London•Vancouver•Melbourne

REINS OF DANGER

Managing Editor: Laura Minchew
Project Editor: Beverly Phillips

Library of Congress Cataloging–in–Publication Data

Janney, Rebecca Price, 1957–
      Reins of danger/ Rebecca Price Janney.
            p.   cm.— (The Heather Reed mystery series; #8)
      "Word kids!"
            Summary: When Heather and her best friend go to California
to watch the Olympic equestrian trials, they encounter a plot to
sabotage the competition, destroy some elite thoroughbred horses,
and take over the prestigious Spencer Wood horse farm.
      ISBN 0–8499–3632–2
      [1. Mystery and detective stories. 2. Horses—Fiction. 3. Olym-
pics—Fiction.   4. Horsemanship—Fiction.]
I. Title.   II. Series: Janney, Rebecca Price, 1957–   Heather Reed
mystery series; #8.
PZ7.J2433Re   1995
[Fic]—dc20   94–43616
                                                                    CIP
                                                                     AC

Printed in the United States of America

95 96 97 98 99 LBM 9 8 7 6 5 4 3 2 1

REINS OF DANGER is dedicated to For the Moment *and all his friends at Vintage Farm, especially Karen Golding, Maggie Mulligan, and two-time Olympian Michael Matz.*

Contents

1

And They're Off!

Y ou don't mean it!" Heather Reed jumped up from her chair.

"Oh, but I do!" her best friend Jenn McLaughlin returned, her blue eyes dancing. "It's true, isn't it, Mom?"

Mrs. Wendy McLaughlin was pleased that Jenn's suggestion had gone over so well. "I've already spoken to my sister. She and her husband think it's a wonderful idea—especially since Jenn's cousin Tiffany will be too busy to keep her company."

"I'd love to go to California with you, Jenn," Heather said. "It sounds so exciting, with your cousin Tiffany training for the Olympics and all."

Tiffany Blake, Jenn's eighteen-year-old cousin, had been riding horses since she was old enough to walk. Now she was about to compete in a ten-day trial for the U.S. Olympic Equestrian Team.

"It certainly is exciting," Mrs. McLaughlin agreed.

"For me, too," Jenn's little brother Geoff intruded as

he passed through the kitchen. "I get to use her room while she's gone."

"Yeah, just don't even think of moving your tarantula into it," his red-headed sister warned as he walked out the door.

Geoff's room was going to be part of the McLaughlin's summer remodeling project. Mrs. McLaughlin shook her head with a laugh. "Anyway, Heather, I hate to see Jenn fly out to California by herself."

"Me, too," her daughter echoed. "I've never been on a plane before."

"I'd love to go. You know how much I've been wanting to ride horses lately, Jenn," Heather said. "All I have to do is talk Mom and Dad into it."

"That's where I can help," Mrs. McLaughlin smiled.

That night after dinner, Jenn and her parents joined Heather and her mom and dad, plus Heather's older brother, Brian, in the Reeds' family room. As Mrs. Reed poured iced tea and passed a plate of chocolate chip cookies, Jenn's mother explained the situation.

"I'm not saying we won't let Jenn go if Heather can't make it," she pointed out. "It's a family tradition that the East Coast cousins visit the West Coast cousins for the entire summer when they turn sixteen, and vice versa."

Jenn interrupted. "Remember when my sister, Amy, went four years ago, and when Tiffany came here two years later?"

"Yes, I remember that your cousin was a delightful young woman," Heather's mother said.

"I remember her, too," Brian joked.

Jenn looked hurt. Ever since she had known him, she had had a crush on Brian. So far, though, he'd never even noticed her, except as his little sister's friend.

Then Mr. McLaughlin spoke up. "It's just that we'd feel better if Heather could be with Jenn those first couple of weeks."

Brian started to say something sarcastic about how much trouble his detective-sister could get into but decided against it when he caught a sideways glance from his dad. Heather held her breath as her parents searched each other's expressions to see what the other was thinking.

"You don't need to tell us right now," Mr. McLaughlin offered, to Heather's disappointment. "Think it over if you need some time."

"Actually, we don't need to," Mr. Reed responded. "Heather, if you'd like to go, you may."

His excited daughter ran to her parents and hugged them. "Oh, thank you so much!"

"Yes," Mrs. McLaughlin chimed in. "Thank you."

After two busy weeks of preparation, Heather and Jenn found themselves spurting out of a crowded plane like Jonah from the whale. The girls struggled down the ramp toward the terminal under the weight of their overstuffed carry-on bags. People ahead of them were already in their loved ones' arms or shaking hands with business associates.

Jenn's face lit up as she spotted her Aunt Sharon. The woman's attractive face glowed as she first embraced Jenn, then Heather. Although she hadn't seen Sharon Blake since she was six, Heather immediately felt comfortable with her. *She looks a lot like Jenn's mom,* she thought.

"Where's Tiffany?" Jenn asked her aunt.

"Uh, she couldn't make it." Mrs. Blake looked a bit nervous. "Let's go get your suitcases," she hurried to say. "Where are they?"

After Heather mentioned the correct baggage claim area, she and Jenn followed Mrs. Blake there. *I wonder what's up with Tiffany,* the teenage sleuth wondered as they walked through the noisy terminal. *Jenn's aunt seems upset about something.*

Although Heather was still in high school, she had a reputation for being a bright amateur detective. She had already solved seven difficult cases that had baffled adults twice her age. Now Heather was hoping to find a mystery to solve in California.

She and Jenn claimed their luggage and wheeled it in a cart to the passenger-pickup area outside. Mrs. Blake fumbled in her purse for her car keys.

"Oh, I hope I didn't lock them in the station wagon," she moaned. "I have such a bad habit of doing that." After several tense moments, Mrs. Blake pulled out the rattling key chain and smiled. "There! I'll go after the car while you stay here with the suitcases," she announced.

Heather and her friend waited at the curb, watching the swaying palm trees.

"It's so beautiful," Jenn sighed happily, "even with all this commotion."

"It sure is," Heather said.

"I wonder why Tiffany didn't come," Jenn was puzzled because her aunt hadn't given an explanation.

"That does seem strange, doesn't it?" Heather reflected.

On the way to San Clemente, which was a little over an hour's drive from the airport, Jenn asked her aunt about Tiffany. "I thought she was coming to meet us."

Mrs. Blake exhaled slowly. Some moments later, she said, "Tiffany had planned to, and she's very sorry she couldn't make it."

"What happened?" Jenn persisted.

"Tiffany's had a rough couple of days," she said. "One of Spencer Wood Farm's top show horses nearly died Saturday night."

"Oh, no!" Jenn exclaimed. "It wasn't Surfer Girl, was it?"

Her aunt shook her head. "No, it was Arabian Knight, whose rider is Melanie Cutler. Surfer Girl has had her own problems, though."

"Isn't Melanie Cutler another top show-jumper?"

"Yes," Mrs. Blake said. "She's hoping to get an Olympic spot, too. There are only five to be had and . . ." Jenn's Aunt Sharon cut herself off.

Heather sat a little forward, intrigued by the story, wondering why Jenn's aunt wouldn't say more about Melanie Cutler. "That's really too bad about the horse," she said after a few moments. "What happened?"

"He got colic." The attractive woman frowned deeply.

"What's that?" Heather questioned.

"It's a fairly common stomach disorder," Mrs. Blake explained.

"What causes it?" Jenn asked.

"Anything from overwork to moldy hay or too much grass. Horses love to graze, and if they're left out too long, they'll eat too much."

"Mrs. Blake, you said that Surfer Girl has had problems, too. Like what?" asked Heather.

"She's been acting really crazy." She shook her head sadly. "Spencer Wood Farm really has been going downhill since Mr. Spencer had a stroke two years ago."

"Does Brad still work there?" Jenn questioned. Her cousin Brad was Tiffany's fifteen-year-old brother.

"Yes," she sighed. "He was an assistant to the stable manager, Tori Caine. But then the groom quit, and Brad's filling in until a permanent one can be found," Mrs. Blake answered. "For the life of him, he can't figure out why these things are happening."

There was an uncomfortable silence. "What do you think is going on?" Heather asked.

"Who knows," Jenn's aunt sighed again. "Some people are blaming the staff, including Brad, for being careless. The problems shouldn't be happening, though—not if the horses have had proper care."

"But Brad's so good with horses," Jenn defended her cousin.

"He sure is. I just hope everything settles down by next week when the trials begin. If Tiffany hopes to become an Olympic team member, she's going to have to prove herself then."

"How does that selection process work?" asked Heather.

"Well, there are trials that take place," the woman began. "They involve a series of seven classes, or competitions. Every four years they're held in a different region of the country. This time, of course, the trials are at various places around California. The judges choose the ten riders and horses with the cleanest rounds and the top scores."

"What do you mean by a round?" asked Heather, deeply interested.

"Each horse and rider have just under ninety seconds to jump a series of obstacles. The round is considered clean if the horse doesn't knock over any planks that make up the obstacle fences," Mrs. Blake explained. "Every time the horse knocks one over, it's called a fault, and four points are automatically given. Then, if the horse refuses to jump an obstacle, that's three points. The goal is to get zero points and finish under ninety seconds."

"Sounds challenging," Heather commented.

"It is," Mrs. Blake nodded. "Anyway, when the top ten riders are chosen, they compete for four spots. The fifth best becomes the Olympic team alternate. Next week's competition in San Juan Capistrano is the first trial."

"Do you think Arabian Knight will be well enough to compete by then?" Heather asked.

"No one knows yet," Mrs. Blake shrugged. "Colic can be mild or life-threatening. We don't know just yet how serious Arabian Knight's condition is." After a brief pause she added, "You know, horses aren't nearly as strong as people think. They have a lot of weight to carry on legs thinner than ours."

Heather had never thought of that before.

"So Tiffany is really upset about this horse?" Jenn asked.

"Yes, but it's not only that," her Aunt Sharon replied. "Her own horse's wildness disturbs her, too. And much worse than that is what happened to Rick Spencer. Do you remember him, Jenn?"

"The son of the farm's owner?" she asked.

"That's right." Jenn's aunt inhaled sharply. "He was shot last night."

2

Jumping to Conclusions

Jenn's blue eyes widened in alarm. "What happened to him?"

"Rick was driving his fiancée home. At a red light someone tried to rob them. When Rick resisted, he was shot," Mrs. Blake shuddered.

"Oh, how awful!" Jenn remarked. "How badly was he hurt?"

"The bullet grazed his neck," she answered. "Thank God it didn't do any permanent damage." Jenn's aunt glanced at Heather in the rearview mirror. "Does this sound like a mystery?"

"It sure does," Heather answered. "Have the police caught the attacker?"

"No," Mrs. Blake shook her head. "But my husband Roger is a captain on the local police force, and he told me that they have a rough description of the robber. That is, they know his approximate size. But he was wearing a nylon stocking over his face and a dark watchman's cap."

9

"So, the police know it was a man?" the teenager followed up.

Sharon Blake seemed rattled. "That's what Roger said."

"Maybe the robber spoke during the hold-up," Heather reflected.

"Is she always this quick?" Jenn's aunt asked in amazement. Her niece grinned broadly.

"I told you she was awesome," Jenn said.

A short time later, Mrs. Blake got off the freeway and steered the cream-colored station wagon down streets lined with palm trees and brightly-colored stucco houses.

"I think it's beautiful here!" Heather exclaimed.

"Thank you," her hostess smiled.

"I love the red tile roofs," Jenn marveled. "Are they all like that?"

"Mostly," her aunt said. "The fire codes are very strict because it's often so dry here. We go weeks and weeks without rain. Wildfires are common and can easily get out of control."

She pulled into a sloping driveway a few minutes later. Beautiful pots of colorful flowers graced the multi-level, brick terrace leading to the spacious stucco house. A teenager was working under the hood of a Volkswagen Beetle.

"That's my cousin, Brad," Jenn told Heather as they got out of the car.

"Jenn!" the young man exclaimed. He came over and

went to hug her, then stopped suddenly. "My hands are greasy. Sorry."

"No problem," Jenn laughed. "Brad, this is my best friend, Heather Reed. Heather, Brad Blake."

They exchanged nice-to-meet-you's, then Brad excused himself. "I'll go wash my hands, and then I'll help with the luggage. If you travel like my sister, I'm in for a workout." In spite of his pleasant greeting, Brad seemed a little tense.

It must be the pressure he's under at the farm, Heather thought.

"Speaking of your sister, where is she?" Mrs. Blake asked.

"Still inside. She's pretty upset," he said quietly.

"Will you excuse me, girls?" Aunt Sharon asked her guests.

"Sure," they said together.

Brad returned a few minutes later to help carry their suitcases. Once inside, Heather felt right at home with the cheerful country decor and large windows. A huge, eat-in kitchen stretched along the entire left side of the first floor. It was separated from the right side by a wooden staircase and an open foyer that looked like a flower shop. Behind the kitchen, the family room hosted a brick fireplace and an entertainment center. Down the hall to the right were three bedrooms, Tiffany's, the guest suite, and a sewing room. Mrs. Blake led her visitors to their room. It had an antique four-poster bed pushed up against a window.

"I can see the ocean from here!" Jenn cried out.

Heather pushed closer to the window to catch a glimpse. "Oh, it's beautiful!" she exclaimed.

"From upstairs you can see it much better," Aunt Sharon pointed out.

"Hi," came a shy voice from the hallway. Tiffany Blake had emerged from her bedroom across the hall. Although she had pretty face, it looked as if she had been crying.

"Tiffany!" Jenn squealed. Her cousin's tear-stained face brightened as they hugged. "You remember Heather, don't you?"

"I do," she said politely. "Hi."

"Hi, Tiffany." They exchanged an awkward hug.

"We heard about the horse and Rick," Jenn said quietly.

The eighteen-year-old didn't know what to say. After a pause, she told them, "I'm really sorry I didn't come to meet your plane."

"We understand," Heather reassured her.

Just then the phone rang, and Brad scooted into Tiffany's room to answer it. "It's for you, Tiff," he announced. "It's Kim."

Tiffany rushed toward the phone and began talking quickly. Brad explained, "Kim Rosen is Rick Spencer's fiancée. She's really nice."

A few minutes later, Tiffany returned. "Kim says Rick is doing much better today."

"That's wonderful!" her mother said.

"She says he's really antsy, though. Mom, I want to

visit him. Would that be okay even though we have company?"

"It's up to them," Aunt Sharon offered.

Tiffany suddenly had a bright idea. "Would you two like to go with me? The hospital's near the ocean, and we could walk on the beach afterward."

Jenn and Heather had hoped to rest after the long flight, but the thought of seeing the ocean renewed their energy. Before leaving, though, they called their parents to let them know they had arrived safely.

When the teens got into the station wagon, Tiffany started talking about Spencer Wood Farm's troubles. "Mr. Spencer's only sixty-seven, but he had a nasty stroke two years ago," she said. "He used to oversee every aspect of the farm from buying horses to managing competitions, but all that's changed. His wife, who's several years younger, is so busy taking care of him that she doesn't get involved much with the horses."

"What about Rick?" Jenn asked. "Hasn't he taken over for his dad?"

"Well, sort of. But he and the trainer, Jon Kent, have had some clashes over how things should be done and who's in charge. For example, Rick wants to buy horses from farms his dad has dealt with for years, and Jon wants to experiment. Everybody knows Rick pulls more weight since he's the owner's son, but Jon's always talking about how much more experienced he is." Tiffany sighed. Then she added, "The truth is, Rick's an excellent horseman. He even took an individual bronze medal at the Barcelona Olympics in 1992."

"Wow," Heather said from the back seat. "That's impressive."

"That's another sore spot between Rick and Jon," Tiffany mentioned. "Although Jon trained really hard to make the Olympic team in 1980, the U.S. boycotted the games that year. Unfortunately, sometimes Rick throws that back at Jon when they're arguing."

"How long has Jon been the trainer?" Heather asked.

"Oh, about eight years," Tiffany waved a hand expressively.

"Has there been a problem all that time?" Jenn questioned.

"Not exactly," her cousin said slowly. "At first Jon and Mr. Spencer worked well together. Mr. Spencer has had some of the best show horses in America, and Jon was happy to train them and their riders. Little by little, though, Jon started doing things his way, like hiring people without consulting Mr. Spencer. That didn't go over too well, either."

"So, Jon Kent saw his opportunity to take charge when Mr. Spencer got sick?" Heather guessed.

"Uh-huh," Tiffany nodded.

"That sounds pretty tense," Jenn remarked.

Heather asked Tiffany to describe the incident with Arabian Knight.

"That's another sad story," she said, steering the wagon through traffic.

"How did he get sick?"

"It seems that someone's been letting him graze too long, and too much grass can make a horse sick. Plus, Brad has found moldy hay in Arabian Knight's stall. Unfortunately someone who I believe is innocent is getting blamed for it."

"What happened?" Heather asked eagerly.

"There's a young woman in her twenties who works with the horses," Tiffany began. "Her name is Abby Valeet. She's so sweet and loves Arabian Knight to death. But she is slightly learning disabled. And sometimes she forgets to go home at night because she's so interested in him. Several times we've found her sleeping in the barn the next day."

"Why in the world would she be a suspect?" Jenn asked. "I mean, if she likes the horses so much."

"It doesn't make any sense, does it? But, you see, Abby was around Arabian Knight constantly the day before he got really sick. Jon says we can't risk keeping her on board. He thinks she was forgetting to bring Arabian Knight in from grazing and not keeping his hay fresh."

"Did he fire her?" Heather asked.

"Yes. I'll bet Abby is heartbroken, too. She loved that horse even more than Melanie did. Melanie's his rider." After a long pause, Tiffany said, "You know what's really weird?"

"No, what?" asked her companions.

"Abby told Jon that during the night, a loud noise woke her up. When she looked up and toward the entrance of the barn, she saw a phantom horse with a rider whose long hair glowed in the moonlight!"

3

Obstacle Course

That creeps me right out!" Jenn shivered.

It made Heather's skin crawl, too. "What happened?"

Tiffany shrugged as she stopped for a red light near the hospital parking lot. "Abby told me she didn't stick around long enough to find out."

"Where did she go?" Heather persisted.

"Home. Abby lives about a mile and a half from Spencer Wood Farm. No one I've talked to believes it really happened." Tiffany smiled. "Abby does have a vivid imagination, but I'm inclined to believe something scared her away, whatever it was."

At the hospital's information desk an elderly volunteer told them Rick Spencer was on the seventh floor. As they headed for the elevator, Tiffany pointed to a staircase on the right. "I haven't had much exercise today," she said. "Let's take the stairs."

"I'll take the elevator," Jenn responded. "I've had *plenty* of exercise today!"

"I'm with Jenn," Heather grinned. "Do you mind?"

"Not at all," Tiffany answered. "See you in a minute."

"You know, Heather," Jenn said in the elevator, "I'm getting very hungry—in spite of the yucky hospital smells."

Heather checked her watch. It was still set to Eastern Standard Time. "No wonder!" she pointed out. "It's six-thirty-five back home, and that means it's dinnertime."

Jenn groaned. "I don't think we'll be eating for another two hours at least. It's only three-thirty-five here." A moment later she made a suggestion. "While Tiffany's visiting this Rick guy, let's go to the snack shop. She can meet us there when she's finished."

At first Heather didn't respond. Although she felt her stomach rumble, too, she was hoping to speak briefly with Rick Spencer about the shooting. "Maybe," she said simply.

They rejoined Tiffany shortly afterward, and Jenn shared the snack shop idea with her.

"I'm sure you must be famished," Tiffany sympathized, "but I'd really like you to stay with me while I visit Rick. I not only want you to meet him, but," she lowered her voice and blushed, "I'm a little nervous. Hospitals do that to me."

"Okay," her cousin said slowly.

"Thanks!" Tiffany glowed. "I'll take you somewhere much better than the snack shop when we finish. The visit won't take more than a few minutes."

Heather liked this idea. She and Jenn followed Tiffany to Rick's room as Jenn poked about in her backpack.

Finally she produced a chocolate bar with a worn wrapper. "Anybody want some?" She waved it in front of Heather and Tiffany. They encouraged her to have it all.

"Here it is," Tiffany pointed to Rick Spencer's room.

They paused and could hear people talking inside. *It sounds like they're not getting along very well,* Heather thought. *I wonder what's going on.*

Unfortunately she couldn't tell because the constant announcements rolling over the public address system drowned out the conversation. Shortly after the girls arrived and Jenn had polished off her chocolate bar, two people emerged from Rick's private room. One was a petite woman in her twenties. She had a peaches-and-cream complexion and blonde hair that was short and wavy.

Her companion towered over her at six-feet-two. He appeared to be in his late thirties with a tanned, leathery face and a lean build. His dark blond hair was slightly wind-blown.

"He looks like a middle-aged surfer," Jenn whispered in Heather's ear.

"I was just trying to be nice," the man said, spreading his hands.

"I doubt that's possible." Her blue eyes looked accusing. *She's British,* Heather noted the woman's accent.

"Oh, hello, Tiffany," the man said as he turned to leave.

"Jon," she said awkwardly.

The woman turned on her heels and went back into the room.

"Who are your friends?" Jon asked Tiffany.

"This is my cousin, Jenn McLaughlin, and her friend, Heather Reed," she explained. "They just flew in from Philadelphia. Jenn, Heather, this is Jon Kent, my trainer."

Closer up, Heather thought he looked tired. His eyes were slightly puffy.

"Nice to meet you," he said, shaking their hands.

"How is he?" Tiffany nodded toward Rick's room.

"He seems much better," Jon smiled. "See for yourself."

Then the trainer politely excused himself and hurried to the elevator. *That was sure strange,* Heather thought. *I wonder why Jon and that woman had words?* Heather followed Tiffany and Jenn into the room. The drapes were drawn, and it was gloomy. Rick Spencer lay in bed, looking weary from his ordeal.

"Rick, love, Tiffany Blake is here to see you," the woman said, hovering over him. She appeared eager to smooth whatever unpleasantness had just happened. However, even without Jon Kent there, the mood in Rick's room was still pretty strained.

"Tiffany," he said weakly. "I'm so glad you came."

She moved next to Rick and kissed him on the forehead. "How are you feeling?" she asked, sounding afraid and shy.

"Better," he managed a grin. "Much better."

"Thank God," she answered.

"Tiffany brought some friends with her," the beautiful woman told Rick.

"Who are they?" he wanted to know.

Tiffany repeated the same introductions she'd given to Jon Kent. Only this time, she concluded with, "Jenn and Heather, I'd like you to meet Rick Spencer and his fiancée, Kim Rosen."

Everyone said hello, and Rick squeezed their hands with a much stronger grip than Heather imagined possible for a man in his weakened condition. A clumsy silence followed in which everyone tried to act normal but couldn't.

"Well, we'll be going now," Tiffany told Rick, shifting her weight from foot to foot. "We don't want to tire you. Besides, I need to find some food for Jenn and Heather. According to their stomach clocks, it's past dinner."

"Thanks for coming, Tiff," Rick said. "Please come again."

"I will," she promised. "I'll be praying that you get better real soon."

"Thanks. Keep training hard. You're the best."

"I'll walk you outside," Kim offered, and she followed them into the hallway. "I'm so glad you came," she said in her British accent.

"Thank *you*," Tiffany responded. "I hope you didn't mind my bringing company."

"Not at all," she smiled. Then she asked politely, "How was your flight?"

"Just fine," Heather said, amazed at how Kim was thinking of them in spite of her own difficulties.

"You will be here for the trials, I trust?"

Both sixteen-year-olds nodded. "We can't wait," Jenn said, trying to sound enthusiastic.

"Kim, I don't mean to pry, but is everything okay between you and Jon?" Tiffany inquired, assuming it was not.

Kim gave a little snort and looked down at the floor. "I'm afraid Rick got upset when Jon came."

"More of the same?"

"I guess," Kim said mysteriously.

Something else is going on here, Heather considered, *something Kim is reluctant to talk about.*

Jenn's nervousness became apparent when she started babbling. "Tiffany told us everything that's been going on at Spencer Wood Farm with Mr. Spencer's stroke, Rick and Jon's disagreement, Arabian Knight's illness, the phantom horse, and the hold-up."

Tiffany's face went crimson.

"Yes, it has been quite a mystery," Kim said graciously.

"It's good that we came, then, because Heather Reed is a great amateur detective. I'm sure she can figure everything out," Jenn continued.

"It's true," Tiffany said. "My Aunt Wendy, Jenn's mother, sends me newspaper clippings about the cases Heather's solved." Heather's face reddened slightly as she noticed the searching way in which Kim Rosen regarded her.

"Perhaps we shall need your services," she said politely.

"I'll be glad to help in any way I can," Heather replied.

"Well, we'll be going now," Tiffany interrupted. "These girls are really hungry and jet-lagged."

"That's for sure," Jenn said wryly.

Minutes later, Heather let the pounding surf and the laughter of sunbathers fill her mind as she and her friends had a snack at a sidewalk café across from the ocean.

"This is incredible!" Jenn kept repeating. "I wonder if I could get my family to move out here. I'd love sunshine like this year-round."

"We do have a rainy season," Tiffany said as she sipped iced tea.

"Not like ours, though," Jenn huffed. "We've had some nasty weather on the East Coast lately."

"Yeah, but we have earthquakes," Tiffany grinned.

It was obvious Jenn had forgotten about the quakes. She suddenly stopped chewing her ham and cheese croissant and swallowed hard. The other two laughed.

The teenagers returned to the Blake home following a short walk along the beach. On the way there, Tiffany pointed out a bike path that she often used to go from her house to the shore. "It's just two miles from our front door to the beach," she said.

It was five-thirty when the teenagers walked through the front door. Sharon Blake encouraged Heather and Jenn to lie down until it was time for dinner. "I'm sure you girls must be exhausted."

"I'm starting to be," Heather said.

"What smells so good?" Jenn sniffed.

"Pot roast," her aunt replied.

"Umm, my favorite."

"That's why I made it," Mrs. Blake smiled. "Now, you go take a nap. I'll call you when it's ready."

"Can we help with anything?" Heather volunteered.

"Not for the first forty-eight hours," she said. "After that, you may, but only a little even then. You're here to have fun, not to do chores."

"Isn't she super?" Jenn asked Heather moments later as they stretched out for a nap.

"I like her a lot. Your whole family is nice."

"How 'bout that Rick Spencer? I thought he was so cool, even though he was sick."

"I thought he was good-looking, too," Heather admitted.

"Those clear blue eyes, and the stubbly beard, and the shaggy hair," Jenn said dreamily.

"I'll tell Pete!" Heather threatened, referring to Pete Gubrio, a guy Jenn dated back in Kirby, Pennsylvania.

The teenagers threw pillows at each other, then lay down again for a short nap. Just before six-fifteen, Tiffany knocked on the door and opened it softly. "Heather?" she asked. "Are you awake?"

"Uh-huh," she muttered.

"Someone from the airline is on the phone asking for you."

"For me?" Heather asked dumbly.

"Yes. You can use the phone in my room."

Heather rolled out of bed slowly so as not to disturb Jenn. *Who in the world could be calling me,* she wondered. Heather padded across the hall in her bare feet and picked up the phone. Tiffany discreetly left the room, closing the door behind her.

"Hello?" Heather asked sleepily. She thought she heard the person say something about the beach. "Excuse me? I just woke up, and I'm having trouble understanding you."

"Come to the beach," the caller said. "Make it early tomorrow, and come alone."

4

By Dawn's Early Light

Heather's skin tingled. "Who is this?" she demanded.

"Heather, this is Kim Rosen."

This came as a surprise to the teenage detective. "What can I do for you?"

"I must see you tomorrow morning."

"Why?"

"I can't say now, but please don't let me down," Kim pleaded. "I have to talk to you."

"All right," Heather consented. "Where and what time?"

"I'll be at the San Clemente pier with my fishing tackle. Bring yours, too, just in case," she advised.

"In case what?" Heather asked, wondering where she'd get fishing equipment in the first place.

"Oh, I can't say now. Just come, please," the young woman begged.

"All right," Heather consented. "What time?"

"Seven o'clock," Kim requested. "Thank you so much." There was a slight pause, then she added,

"Don't bring anyone with you, and don't tell anyone I called."

Heather's hand trembled slightly as she put down the receiver. *What in the world is going on?* she wondered. *And where in the world am I going to get a fishing pole, or get to the pier at all, let alone without anyone knowing?*

A few minutes later, Heather wandered into the kitchen for a glass of water. Mrs. Blake was putting the finishing touches on dinner as Brad set the table and Tiffany prepared lemonade.

"What did you tell him?" Mrs. Blake asked Heather.

"Tell who?" Heather asked.

"That guy from the airline who just called."

"Uh, nothing special," she stammered.

"They just started doing that," Mrs. Blake said, lifting a saucepan of fresh peas from the stove. "I got called once, too. I guess they want to make sure your flight was satisfactory. There's such competition among airlines."

"Yes, there is," Heather responded. *Boy, that was close!* she thought. *Kim must have disguised her voice or had a man call for her, pretending to be from the airline.*

Five minutes later a sleepy-eyed Jenn rambled into the large kitchen just as her Uncle Roger came home from work wearing his police uniform.

"Jenn!" he cried out, opening his arms for a hug. She rushed over to accept his warm greeting.

"It's great seeing you!" she exclaimed.

"Same here," he smiled. "You've grown so much since we last saw you. Your mom and dad send pictures, but still. . . ." Then he turned to Jenn's friend. "You must be Heather." He held out his hand, and she shook it.

"Hello, Mr. Blake," Heather said politely. "Thank you for inviting me."

"Well, we're mighty glad you came."

As Jenn's uncle greeted his wife and kids, Heather took stock of him. He was tall and on the hefty side with a neatly-trimmed beard and mustache. *Tiffany obviously got her light hair from her mom,* Heather observed. *Brad's is dark, like his dad. Mr. Blake looks like the outdoors-type. I bet he has a fishing pole I could borrow.*

Before her father went upstairs to change his clothes, Tiffany told him about Rick's progress. A few minutes later, they all sat down to the mouth-watering meal Mrs. Blake had prepared. A cool breeze started blowing in from the back patio, and Heather shivered in her tee-shirt.

"I thought California would be warmer than this," she said.

"It's pretty cool along the coast," Mr. Blake remarked.

"It's really hot in the desert, though," Brad said. "I heard it got up to 112 degrees today."

"Wow!" Jenn exclaimed. "I don't think I want to go there."

"It's beautiful, Jenn," Tiffany smiled.

"It only gets into the seventies here on most summer

days," Mrs. Blake said. "The mornings and nights are usually in the fifties, so you'll need a jacket or sweater."

I'd better dress warmly tomorrow morning, the teenage sleuth noted mentally. "My dad would love your fishing pier," she said a few minutes later, hoping to find out indirectly whether her host had any equipment.

"Is that right?" Mr. Blake asked.

"Do you fish?" she pursued.

"I sure do." He leaned back in his chair. "I've even caught some shark and a sting ray there."

"That's enough of your fish stories," his wife said, getting up from the table. As she cleared their dinner plates to make way for cherry pie with vanilla ice cream, Mr. Blake told Heather and Jenn that there was plenty of fishing gear in the garage in case they got the urge to go to the pier.

Great! Heather thought. *That solves one problem.*

"We have bikes you can use, too," Brad added.

That solves my other problem, Heather smiled to herself.

By nine o'clock, the two East Coast teens were ready for bed. "I'm so sleepy I can hardly keep my eyes open," Jenn complained as they sat in the living room watching old family videos. Heather hadn't been paying much attention, since her mind was focused on the new mystery.

"According to your time, it's midnight," Tiffany said.

"Go to bed, girls," Mrs. Blake advised, clicking off the TV. "We can watch these another time."

"Oh, joy," Brad muttered, rising from the couch. "I'm

going upstairs to see if I got any e-mail today," he called over his shoulder.

"Don't stay on the computer too long," his dad advised. "I need to use it."

Heather and Jenn washed up and put on their pajamas, then slipped into the comfortable bed. A gentle breeze blew through their open window as Heather prayed that she'd wake up in time to meet Kim Rosen at seven. She didn't dare use the alarm on her wrist watch because it might awaken Jenn.

The following morning Heather was up at five-thirty, encouraged that she hadn't overslept. *It seems as if everyone's still asleep,* she concluded after listening for movement in the house. The sixteen-year-old left a note on the bathroom sink saying that she had gone for a bike ride. Then she slipped on a pair of jeans and a sweatshirt. After she laced up her tennis shoes and grabbed her backpack, Heather tip-toed out the door. Jenn was snoring gently, oblivious to her friend's movements.

Heather went to the side door to the garage and found it unlocked. While reaching for a light switch, she knocked over a clay pot. Moving quickly, she caught it in midair, but a pair of grass clippers slipped from a wire rack and clattered to the floor. Heather's heart pounded as she imagined Mr. Blake racing to the garage with his gun, ready to arrest a burglar. When that didn't happen, she took a quick inventory of the garage. There were wet suits, a motorboat, and an array of sporting equipment, including five bicycles and eight fishing poles. Heather selected an older mountain bike and a retractable fishing pole that fit in her backpack and took off for the bike path behind the house.

If it hadn't been for her uneasiness, she would have lost herself in the beauty of the coastal California dawn with its pinks and yellows as the grayish surf throbbed in the distance. Heather soon arrived at the bustling pier where dozens of fishermen had already gathered. The pungent odors of caught fish, bait, and salt air attacked the teenager's senses. She stopped briefly to buy some bait, then forged on, searching for Kim Rosen. Finally, Heather saw Kim dressed in a fashionable sweat suit and looking tense.

"Good morning," Heather approached her.

"Hi," Kim said, relaxing. "I was afraid you wouldn't make it." She looked cautiously over her shoulder.

"Are you expecting anyone else?" the teenager asked.

"No," Kim sputtered nervously. "Just you. You didn't tell anyone did you?"

"No."

"Did anyone follow you?"

Heather shook her head.

"How did you get here?"

"I borrowed a bike and used the path," the teenager said.

A few minutes later, she was casting her line over the pier into the gentle waves.

"Heather, are you really as good a sleuth as they say?" Kim asked.

"I do my best," she blushed.

"I realize you're on holiday, but would you be willing to help me . . . I mean, help Rick?"

"Sure," Heather responded.

The breeze ruffled Kim's short, blonde hair, and she sighed heavily. "I thought Rick's conflict with Jon Kent would resolve as Rick took charge of the farm," she began. "But last week Rick and Jon had a terrible argument."

"Were you there?"

"No."

Heather frowned. "How do you know about it, then?"

"There's a girl who works—or rather, worked—for the farm. She was part of a special program for learning disabled people. Her name is Abby Valeet. She told me about it. She said that Rick and Jon nearly came to blows." Kim trembled as she told the unpleasant story. "When I asked Rick about it, he lost his temper and refused to discuss it." Her voice choked. "I've never seen him like that before."

After a brief silence, Heather asked, "Isn't Abby the girl who was fired?"

"Yes. Did Tiffany tell you about her phantom horse?"

"Uh-huh." Heather reeled in her line, thinking she had a bite. It turned out to be only seaweed.

"I think something terrible is happening, Heather," Kim's lower lip quivered.

"Have you tried talking to the Spencers about it?" Heather asked.

"There wouldn't be any use trying," Kim sighed. "Mr. Spencer is still weak, and Mrs. Spencer is completely wrapped up in taking care of him. She's been depending on Rick to handle things." Following a pause she said, "I have a feeling that Jon may have arranged Rick's accident to get him out of the way."

5

Drive-By Menace

How awful!" Heather exclaimed. "What makes you think Jon would do that?"

"A lot is at stake, Heather," Kim explained. "In the world of show horses, there's a good deal of money to be made if you win competitions. If Rick were out of the way, Jon would have full charge over Spencer Wood Farm. If he had enough winning horses and riders, he could become very wealthy."

"Kim, could anyone else be causing the problems at the farm, maybe for different reasons?" Heather asked.

"I'm not sure that I understand."

"Even if Jon did try to get Rick out of the way, what about the problems with the horses, how they're not being cared for properly?" she asked. "That wouldn't be to Jon's benefit if he wants champion horses."

"No, I guess it wouldn't," Kim thoughtfully considered Heather's comments. "Do you really think someone else may be involved?"

"Possibly," Heather reflected. "And it could be for

entirely different reasons." After a few minutes, she asked Kim to describe Rick's encounter with the robber.

"I've been trying to muster up enough courage to tell you the real story," Kim said mysteriously.

"I don't understand," the teenager replied. "Do you mean that Mrs. Blake's version wasn't the truth?"

"She told you only what she knew. The thing is, no one got the real story. Oh, Heather," she sighed. "It's a frightful mess, and Rick swore me to secrecy. He's been so anxious lately, and I'm so afraid our relationship is falling apart." She took a few moments before continuing. "I just have to tell someone or I'll burst!"

Just then a middle-aged man walked up to them, nearly startling them out of their wits. "Catch anything?" he asked pleasantly, peering into Kim's bucket.

"No, we haven't," Heather answered, wondering whether he was an innocent passerby or a suspicious character.

"What kind of bait are you using?" he asked

"Squid," the teenager said shortly.

"Well, squid's all right, but I prefer shrimp," he stated. "You should see the size of the ocean perch I caught here last week with shrimp. I have some extra bait, and I'd be happy to share it."

"No, thank you. We're going to be leaving soon." Heather wished he would go away.

The man plunked down his gear and made himself right at home. "Well, then, I'll give you a hand while you stay," he said.

I think this guy's too forward to be suspicious, Heather decided.

Kim quickly reeled in her line, determined to get as far away from the intruder as possible. Heather followed her example.

"Oh, you girls don't have to go," the man said.

"Yes, we do," Kim said stiffly.

"Well, it was fun. Bye!" he called after them cheerfully.

"What a bother!" Kim exclaimed as she and Heather walked down the pier toward the beach. "He would have to come along just as I was getting courage enough to tell all."

"You don't know him then?" Heather asked.

Kim shook her head impatiently and pointed to a café at the beach end of the pier. "Could we please stop for fifteen minutes and talk over coffee? The restaurant is nearly vacant, so we can speak freely."

"All right," Heather agreed.

Within minutes they had sat down in the outdoor dining area and begun eating their danishes. They were isolated from the other patrons, but Kim still spoke softly.

"What happened to Rick wasn't a hold-up," she began.

"What happened then?" Heather asked, intrigued.

"We were coming back from the farm to my home in San Juan Capistrano that part is true—but we weren't stopped at a light." She sipped her coffee as if to gain courage from it. Kim's hands were trembling. "Rick started sweating, and he kept looking in the rearview mirror. When I asked him what was wrong, he snapped at me."

Heather put down her danish, too absorbed in the story to eat.

"As we slowed for the light, just before we turned into the neighborhood where I live, a red sports car passed us. I started to say something about how dangerously it wove through traffic." She gulped. "Then I saw a stocking-faced man in the car pull a gun. He yelled something nasty at Rick. Then he fired the gun. I screamed as our car lurched across the road. Heather, we narrowly missed an oncoming car! We ended up smashing into a large bush. Before help came, Rick told me to say that it had been a drive-by robbery. He was so agitated that I promised. Today Rick was still insisting I tell that story."

"So, you didn't tell the police the truth?" Heather asked.

"How could I?" Kim asked testily. She was instantly sorry for her tone of voice. "Oh, I do apologize. My nerves are all on edge."

"And with good reason," Heather responded kindly.

"Rick has been so touchy and secretive. I wonder whether there's more here than meets the eye between him and Jon," Kim said. "Do you think you can find out?"

Heather nodded. "I'll try."

"Oh, thank you," she said, gripping Heather's hand. "You mustn't tell anyone what I've told you. Don't even let anyone know that you saw me. Do you understand?"

"I can keep your secret," Heather assured her. "There's

just one thing, though, Kim. We may have to tell the police."

The woman shook her head stubbornly. "No."

"Then I can't help you," Heather said firmly. "At the right time, they'll need to know."

Seeing that she was backed into a corner, Kim relented a bit. "Will you let me decide when that is?"

"I can't promise that, but I won't say anything until I sense that the time is right. Please, Kim, trust me. The police can be more helpful than you can imagine."

"I guess," she said.

"Before I go, I've been wondering something. How do you buy show horses?"

"It depends. Sometimes we go to farms we've dealt with before and ask them if they have what we need. Other times, they come to us," Kim said casually.

"Do you buy them all from the same farms?"

"We generally do. Over the years it's worked out well for the Spencers to stay with certain horse breeders. They know what we need." Kim gave a laugh. "Listen to me—I sound like a Spencer already!"

Heather smiled. "When do you and Rick plan to be married?"

"In October. That is, if Rick is still willing," she added sadly.

"Let's give him the benefit of the doubt until we know more," Heather advised. Kim nodded. "Back to the horse sellers," the teenager said. "Which ones do the Spencers use?"

The blonde thought hard. "There's one near San Diego, and then the others are foreign."

"Which countries?" Heather wanted to know.

"Oh, Germany, France, and Argentina. Over the last year, we've been getting some from Austria. In fact, Surfer Girl, Arabian Knight, and Meridian all came from the same farm in Austria. Jon said they were sure bets as Olympic competitors."

Heather gave a start. "Did you say Austria?"

"Uh-huh."

"I have a friend whose family runs a horse farm there." She was thinking about Katarina Schiller, the intriguing exchange student who had stayed with the Reeds last fall.*

"That's incredible!" Kim exclaimed. "Austria isn't exactly known for its horse farms. I wonder if it's the same one."

"My friend's last name is Schiller," Heather pointed out.

"That's the one!" exclaimed Kim.

"Wow." The teenager thought hard for a moment. "Kim, I'll get in touch with Katarina and ask her if anything strange is going on at her end of things."

"I think that's a wonderful idea," she agreed. "I hope you don't have to wait too long for a response."

Heather had a sudden hunch. "Brad Blake uses e-mail on his computer, and I've got Kat's e-mail address. We often correspond that way."

---

* For more about Katarina Schiller, read *The Exchange Student's Secret*, book number 6 in THE HEATHER REED MYSTERY SERIES.

"That's super!" Kim approved.

"Do you ever sell horses to other farms?" Heather asked a moment later.

"Only on rare occasions."

Heather stood and pulled out her wallet. "Will three dollars cover my meal?"

Kim waved the money away. "It's the least I can do to thank you for helping me and Rick. Do your best, Heather. I don't want to lose him." Then she asked, "Is it okay if I call you again?"

"Sure," Heather said. "By the way, I'm confused about yesterday when you called. How did you do that without giving yourself away? Your accent's pretty distinct."

"I know. I asked a man to tell the Blakes that he was from the airline and was taking a survey about customer satisfaction," Kim blushed. "It sounds ridiculous now, but it was the only thing I could think of."

"It was fine," Heather smiled. "I'll see you around."

"Thank you," Kim said gratefully.

Heather went to her borrowed bike, thankful that no one had stolen it, and headed for the trail. She was deeply concerned about the time. It was now eight-thirty. *No doubt Mr. and Mrs. Blake are up and wondering where I am,* the teenager worried. Then she remembered that Jenn was a late sleeper. *She probably won't be up yet, so the Blakes shouldn't find it unusual that I'm not awake either. They might not have missed me at all!*

Comforted by the thought, Heather followed the bike path as it wound through some streets, weaving carefully through the rush-hour traffic. Her contentment, however, didn't last. The sixteen-year-old got a sinking feeling that someone was following her. Just before she came to a major intersection, the car behind her swerved carelessly, then rammed into the back of her bike. Before she knew what had happened, Heather catapulted through the air!

6

Tension

The sound of screeching brakes pierced the air as the morning traffic halted. Angry onlookers watched in disbelief as the car that struck Heather made a get-away. Heather lay bruised and bleeding in someone's flower bed of pink impatiens. She sat up in a daze while a handful of people hurried over to her.

"Are you hurt badly?" asked a tall woman in a suit.

"I'm not sure," Heather told her.

"What a creep!" a young man with a surfboard announced. "I can't believe he hit you, then took off like that."

"Should we call an ambulance?" inquired an elderly man.

"No, thank you," Heather said.

She tried to get up, and the businesswoman assisted her. "How do you feel?" the lady asked.

"I don't think anything is broken or sprained," the teenager commented, brushing dirt and crushed flowers off her clothes. "I landed on my back, and I think that flower bed and my backpack cushioned the fall." Then she asked anxiously, "Where's my bike?"

The surfer rolled it up to her, struggling because the frame was badly bent. "It's pretty banged up, but I think you can get it fixed. You can't ride it now, though, that's for sure."

"Where are you going?" the businesswoman asked.

"To a neighborhood at the top of the bike path."

"I'll take you there. We can put your bike in my Jeep," she offered.

Heather never accepted rides from strangers, but this was an exception. *I can't ride the bike the way it is, and even if it were working, I'm too sore,* she considered. "I'd like that," she told the woman gratefully.

A few minutes later, Heather found herself in the passenger seat of a late-model Cherokee. The driver turned down her radio and introduced herself. "I'm Barbara Warfield," she said.

"And I'm Heather Reed." Before the woman could ask any more questions, the teenager said, "I'm curious about the person who hit me. Did you see him?"

"To be honest, I was on my car phone and not paying much attention to traffic," Ms. Warfield admitted. "I did catch a glimpse, though, as he plunged through the red light. I was afraid he'd cause another accident."

"You're sure it was a man?" Heather asked.

The woman looked a little embarrassed. "I just made that assumption."

"How about his car? What kind was it?"

"I think it was a blue four-door," Ms. Warfield answered. She didn't find anything unusual about Heather's questions, figuring that the teenager simply wanted to report the incident to the police.

"Foreign or domestic?"

Barbara Warfield shook her head. "That I don't know."

Upon reaching the Blakes', Heather and her driver got the battered mountain bike out. Both Mr. Blake's police car and the station wagon were gone from the driveway. Then the teenager thanked Ms. Warfield for her kindness and went inside, wondering darkly whether the "accident" had been a set-up. *Who knew I would be at that place, at that time?* she thought. Heather suddenly became uneasy. *Kim knew I was going to use the bike path, but why in the world would she have arranged that? Maybe someone was following her and decided to go after me instead,* she decided. *But why?*

Heather put the bike and fishing gear in the garage, then went back to the kitchen. A note lay on the counter near the refrigerator. The teenager picked it up to read. "Dear Jenn and Heather," it began, "So sorry not to be here when you wake up. Hope you slept well. I took Tiffany and Brad to Spencer Wood Farm and plan to return by nine-thirty. Help yourself to breakfast or wait for me, and I'll make something for you. Love, Aunt Sharon."

That was a close call! Heather thought in relief. *They never even knew I was gone. Still, I'll have to tell them about the bike.*

She was eager for a good soak in the bathtub to relieve her stiffness. Before that, however, Heather called the police, praying that Captain Blake didn't answer. Fortunately another officer promised to put an all-points-bulletin in effect for the dangerous driver. Heather didn't say anything about the mystery. Remembering her promise to Kim, she thought, *I'm not ready for that yet, although this could be a first step in drawing the police into this case.*

She hung up the phone and went to her room, opening the door gently. *Jenn's still asleep,* she observed. Heather snatched the note she had left, then quietly gathered her bath items. For a half hour she soaked her aching muscles and bathed her cuts, which helped her feel much better. Back in her room afterward, Heather put on a fresh pair of jeans and a ribbed tee shirt.

"Heather?" Jenn squeaked.

"Good morning," her friend smiled. "Good sleep?"

"Like a baby." Jenn sat up and blinked several times

"Some babies don't sleep well at all," Heather teased.

"This one did!" Jenn picked up the clock on the night stand. "Quarter after nine!" she remarked. "I've been asleep for twelve hours! No wonder I'm hungry. Have you eaten?"

"Just a snack," her friend said, remembering the pastry and coffee at the pier. Heather told her about Mrs. Blake's note.

Jenn stretched. "I think I'll take a quick shower first."

Twenty minutes later the teenagers found Sharon

Blake alone in the kitchen. "Good morning!" she said cheerfully. "Did you eat yet?"

"No," Jenn spoke for both of them.

"How about some Mexican omelettes?" she suggested. "Or would you rather have blueberry pancakes?"

"Umm," her niece moaned pleasantly. "I could do with both."

Her aunt laughed. "Your wish is my command." As she reached into the pantry for pancake mix she said, "I thought that after breakfast, I'd take you to the farm. Would you like that, or do you have something else in mind for your first day here?"

"That would be super," Heather said quickly. *I could look for clues and meet some people involved in this mystery,* she thought excitedly.

"I'd love to see it, too," Jenn added.

A few minutes later as Mrs. Blake poured three glasses of orange juice, Heather mustered the courage to tell her about the bike. "Uh, I have a confession to make," she stammered.

"Oh?" Mrs. Blake raised her eyebrows.

"I woke up early this morning, and I decided to go fishing at the pier," Heather explained.

"I was so out of it I didn't even realize you were gone," Jenn remarked.

Her aunt smiled. "Did you catch anything, Heather?"

"I didn't," she said. "Um, Mrs. Blake, I had a little accident with the bike on my way back."

"Good heavens! Are you all right?" she exclaimed.

"Beside some cuts and bruises, I'm all in one piece," Heather told her. "There's just another thing, though. The bike got banged up."

"How did you get home?" Mrs. Blake asked, far more worried about Heather than the bike.

"A nice lady drove me here. I'm so sorry about the bike," Heather apologized. "I'd like to pay to have it fixed or replaced. It was the blue mountain bike."

"Nonsense!" her hostess exclaimed. "Besides, Brad outgrew it ages ago. Just last week we talked about giving it to the Salvation Army. We weren't even sure they would take it."

"Well, thanks for understanding."

Mrs. Blake looked at Heather pointedly. "If you go out again, please leave a note so I don't worry."

"I will," she promised.

At eleven o'clock, they traveled twenty miles south to Spencer Wood Farm. It took them a half hour to reach it. When they arrived, a mean-looking guard stopped them at the iron gate.

Heather wondered whether he would let them in.

7

Bad Blood

What brings you here?" the man asked.

"My children work here. I brought them earlier, remember?" Mrs. Blake asked with an edge in her voice.

"Oh, right," he murmured, waving them through.

"Jon Kent hired him yesterday," Mrs. Blake pointed out as she drove away. "Normally that gate is wide open, but everyone's on edge," she sighed. "I just hope nothing else goes wrong before the Olympic trials." She didn't seem optimistic.

Heather tingled with anticipation as Jenn's aunt pulled up to a huge barn with parking bays and farm equipment on the outside. Not only did she want to solve the farm's mysteries, she also hoped to go riding during her visit.

"Where does the Spencer family live?" Heather asked as they walked to the main barn.

"See that white stucco building by the palm grove?" Mrs. Blake pointed.

Shielding her eyes from the bright sun, the teenager spotted it in the distance. "It's big."

"They must be loaded!" Jenn exclaimed.

She nearly died of embarrassment when a man said, "Hello, girls." Trainer Jon Kent sat astride a gleaming white horse. He tipped his hat and smiled charmingly.

"Oh, hi, Jon. I'd like you to meet my niece Jenn and her friend Heather," Mrs. Blake said.

"We met at the hospital yesterday." Jon dismounted and removed his leather riding gloves to shake their hands. "I'm so glad you came."

He looks tired, but he's a lot cuter than I remember, Heather reflected. *I guess anyone in riding clothes on a gorgeous horse looks better than in a hospital hallway! I wonder what he's really like.*

"Have you heard anything more about Rick?" Jenn asked.

"He's getting stronger," Jon flashed a dazzling smile as one of the farm's many dogs circled his feet, then ran off.

"Thank God," she commented.

"Listen, I'm on my way to the practice field. Would you like to watch some training?"

"I'd love to!" Jenn exclaimed.

"Me, too," her friend nodded.

While the girls and Mrs. Blake walked next to him as he led his horse, Heather asked some questions. "How many people are training for the Olympics?"

"We have three serious contenders: Tiffany, Melanie Cutler, and Dean Parmi. Just between you and me, I think Tiffany's chances are excellent," he said.

"She has a wonderful trainer," Mrs. Blake smiled. "You

may not know, girls, that Jon was almost in the Olympics himself."

"That's right," Jenn's blue eyes twinkled. "Now when was that?"

"A long time ago," he said.

Heather noticed that Jon had become uncomfortable at the mention of his Olympic history.

"It was 1980," Mrs. Blake said, unmindful of his uneasiness. "Jon made the team, but President Carter boycotted the Moscow games because Russia had invaded Afghanistan."

"Let's go," Jon said abruptly. "I'll show you where the field is."

As they walked there, Heather thought, *I wonder why he doesn't want to talk about missing the Olympics.*

"I'll show you where you can watch," Jon said, trying to sound more cheerful. After taking them to a shaded viewing area, he rejoined his team.

"I think he's adorable," Jenn whispered in Heather's ear.

"You thought Rick was adorable last night," she teased.

"Well, both of them are," the redhead defended herself.

Heather marveled as Melanie Cutler and Dean Parmi's horses jumped the practice fences. Unfortunately, Surfer Girl refused.

"C'mon, girl!" Tiffany urged. "Jump!"

Time after time the stubborn horse would approach a fence, then stop in her tracks. She seemed only to have two speeds—barely idling and full steam ahead.

"What's wrong with Surfer Girl, Aunt Sharon?" Jenn asked.

"She's been a little wild lately, but this is new."

"What's the matter?" Melanie Cutler called out. "Is the poor horsey refusing?"

"Stop it, Melanie!" Tori Caine, the stable manager ordered.

"That Melanie's a piece of work," Jenn commented.

"She's the girl whose horse has colic, and she isn't too happy with her replacement," Mrs. Blake remarked. "Tiffany says she's taking it out on everyone. I think Melanie's been especially hard on my son and daughter, though."

"In what way?" Heather asked.

"She's almost come right out and accused them of making Arabian Knight sick. She thinks they're trying to knock her out of Olympic contention," Mrs. Blake said. "Can you imagine! I know Tiffany and Brad are my kids, and I'm bound to stick by them, but they'd never do something like that."

"Maybe Melanie's accusing them because it's something she might do," Jenn reflected.

"I think that's a good point," Heather agreed. *I'm going to watch this Melanie carefully,* she decided. "How does she get along with Dean Parmi?"

Mrs. Blake gave a snort. "Not much better. He's so aloof, though, that he could care less. He thinks he's too good for lesser mortals than himself."

"How old are most show jumpers?" Heather asked

after a few minutes. Surfer Girl was still refusing to jump.

"There's no typical age," Jenn's aunt explained. "You must be at least eighteen to make the Olympics, but some people compete at that level well into their forties."

They stopped talking as Tiffany coaxed her beautiful horse toward two fences in succession.

"This is important," Mrs. Blake pointed out. "Many horses make it or break it at these set-ups."

Surfer Girl glided over the first jump, and Tiffany's relatives cheered. But their joy didn't last long. Not realizing that there was a second fence, the horse smashed into it, sending Tiffany flying through the air! Heather, Jenn, and Mrs. Blake gasped in horror, then ran toward the fallen girl.

"Are you all right?" her mother asked anxiously.

"My left hand hurts," she moaned in pain. "I broke my fall with it." Bits of grass clung to her clothes and hair.

Jon hurried over to them, and Melanie Cutler trotted nearby on her horse.

"Looks like I'm not the only one with troubles, am I?" she asked sarcastically.

"That's enough Melanie!" Tori Caine yelled.

Melanie rolled her eyes and tossed her ponytail.

"Melanie, you and Dean just keep practicing what we've been going over," Jon told her. Dean Parmi hadn't even stopped to see if Tiffany was okay.

"Tiffany, I know it's upsetting, but don't let Melanie

get to you, honey," Tori soothed. The tall, sturdy woman seemed kind.

Jon lifted Tiffany in his arms and carried her back to the main barn just in case she had hurt something else in her fall. *These aren't exactly the most pleasant people in the world,* Heather told herself as she followed.

A commercial-type truck stood near the entrance of the barn as they approached it. Several horseshoes lay on the ground nearby. The license plate caught Heather's eye with its single word in bold letters, DANSE. *I wonder what that means?* she asked herself.

Then she saw a blacksmith leaning against the vehicle. He pushed back his long, gray hair and sipped coffee from a thermos as the group passed. Inside the barn Brad spotted Jon carrying his sister. "What happened?" he asked in alarm.

"Just a little accident," Jon said as three other workers stopped to see what was going on. "Is Dr. Sandies here yet?"

"Yes."

"Go get her for me, will you?" Jon asked. He kicked open the office door with his right boot and placed Tiffany in a large wooden chair behind the desk. Heather noticed that the walls were lined with mementos of Spencer Wood Farm's glory days. There were two paintings of Rick and his father in their separate Olympic appearances, and glass cases with hundreds of ribbons, most of them blue.

Heather and Jenn watched as a gray-haired woman calmly entered the office.

"Dr. Sandies," Jon said, "Tiffany fell and hurt her hand." As he explained what had happened, the vet examined Jenn's cousin.

"I don't think you broke anything," the doctor pronounced after a few minutes. "If you want to have it x-rayed, you can," she added, "but I don't think it's necessary at this point."

Tiffany agreed.

"Will you wrap it?" Mrs. Blake asked.

"Of course," came the response. "I also recommend some ice for the first few hours as well as muscle relaxants."

"Thank you," Tiffany said politely.

"You're welcome. I'd better get back to Arabian Knight now." Dr. Sandies moved toward the door.

"Is he any better?" Jon questioned.

The vet shook her head as she left.

"Tiffany, are you going to be all right now?" the trainer asked.

"Yes, Jon. Thanks," she responded.

"I'd better get back to the others," he announced and left.

"I'll get you some ice," Brad volunteered.

As they waited, Jenn had a question for her cousin and aunt. "Was that the blacksmith we saw a few minutes ago?"

"Yes," Tiffany managed a smile. "That's Cal Mahoney. In spite of how strange he looks, he's really good." She shook her head in disbelief. "His sunglasses are amazing—round on one side, square on the other!"

"I wonder what his license plate means?" Heather reflected. "It said 'DANSE.'"

"Who knows?" Tiffany shrugged.

"Does he work here full time?" the young sleuth continued.

"No. He hires himself out to various farms."

Mrs. Blake added, "He's the best in this area."

After Brad returned with the ice pack, Jenn spoke again. "You know, I expected the barn to be buzzing with activity, but instead, it's so calm."

Tiffany frowned. "You should've been here earlier. Major upset."

"What do you mean?" Heather asked alertly.

"Horse people are usually pretty sedate. That's because the horses have to be kept composed so they perform better," Tiffany explained. "The animals know when things aren't going well. And they haven't been; that's for sure. Dean Parmi discovered that his horse's leg was sore because his bandages were wrapped too tightly. Dean was furious. Both he and Melanie are now riding substitute horses."

"Why was the horse wearing bandages?" Heather questioned.

"We wrap their legs when they're getting ready for competitions," the eighteen-year-old said. "Anyway, if they're too tight, the bandages hurt the horse's legs. Dean thinks Brad did it on purpose. As if he would!" she defended her brother.

Brad seemed ill at ease. "Dean's just more upset than

usual, Tiff. Let's forget it, okay?" After a pause, he asked Heather and Jenn if they would like a tour of the barn.

"Sure!" they chorused.

"Do you mind, Tiffany?" Jenn asked, concerned.

"Enjoy yourselves," she encouraged them. "I'm just going to rest a little while."

After Brad showed them the tack room, Jenn asked if she and Heather could ride.

"Sure," he said. "I have just the right horses for you and Heather. They're in a different barn."

When they neared the end of the corridor, Heather noticed a lot of activity in one horse's stall. Dr. Sandies was ministering to a sick, black horse as Melanie Cutler watched anxiously. The young rider shot Heather, Jenn, and Brad a dirty look.

"That's Arabian Knight," Brad said quietly. "He's really sick. At least we have the best vet in the district, and she lives close-by, too."

"Really?" Heather asked, also lowering her voice. "Where does Dr. Sandies live?"

"Only two miles away."

"So, Arabian Knight might not make the Olympic trials?" Heather asked softly.

"He might not make it, period," Brad whispered.

"Look!" Jenn exclaimed. "I found something!"

Before Heather and Brad could see what Jenn had found, however, Melanie stepped menacingly toward the redhead.

"Get out of here!" she shouted.

8

The Smell of Danger

Stunned, Jenn moved backward as Melanie balled up her fists. Brad quickly stepped between them. Dr. Sandies had the final say.

"Melanie Cutler, you either control your anger or leave," she ordered. "Arabian Knight isn't going to get better with his rider acting like a madwoman."

Melanie gave Jenn another nasty look and stormed out of the barn. "Let's get out of here," Brad suggested. He took his cousin by the elbow and led her toward a different barn where other horses stayed.

"I think she's crazy!" Jenn shuddered when they got outside. "All I did was find a hair scrunchie, and she went ballistic."

"Let me see it," Heather requested. She turned the object over in her hands, admiring its tapestry design in rich shades of red, blue, green, and gold.

"Do you think it's a clue?" Jenn questioned.

"It could be, especially because Melanie got so upset when you found it."

Brad looked confused. "What does it mean?"

"It's possible that Melanie has been tampering with her own horse. She may have been wearing this scrunchie at the time," Heather reflected.

"Why would she do a thing like that?" Brad asked, amazed.

"That, I don't know, but her behavior isn't exactly normal." Heather turned to her friend. "Mind if I keep this, Jenn?"

"I don't want it, that's for sure," she snorted.

When they got to the smaller barn, Brad began saddling up two beautiful horses for the girls to ride. Heather's was a black mare with a white blaze on its nose.

"This is Solar Wind," he said. "Jenn, you'll have Master Mind."

"Is he gentle?" the teenager asked, stroking the gray horse's mane.

"He'll be fine. But you and Heather both need to keep the horses at a slow walk since you're not experienced riders."

"Will you go with us, Brad?" Heather asked. "I'd like it if you showed us around the farm."

"I guess I could take a short break," he said.

As it turned out, Spencer Wood Farm proved to be much larger than Heather had first realized. There were several barns and other assorted out-buildings, along with five different practice fields. Because of Heather's bike accident, bouncing on the horse made her sore muscles ache. She didn't protest, though. The teenager wanted to learn as much about the farm as she could.

On their return trip to the barns, Heather noticed something she hadn't seen before. "What's that doing there?" she asked Brad, pointing to a silver trailer in a grove of palm trees.

"That's another of our unsolved mysteries," he remarked.

"What do you know about it?" Heather asked eagerly as they stopped and Solar Wind bent down to eat some grass.

"This guy has been living there since right before Mr. Spencer had his stroke. Rick told us to ignore him, that he was a family friend. He's really mysterious, though," Brad commented. "He takes early morning walks, and sometimes we run into each other. But he never even looks at me. No one seems to know his name or where he came from."

"Rick said he was a family friend, though," Heather pointed out.

"I know, but I think there's more to it than that."

"Like what?" she persisted.

"There's been talk about whether he's the one sabotaging our horses," he stated. "He's in a perfect position to do it."

Heather thought about this for a moment. "It seems odd, though, that the Spencers' friend would try to destroy their business."

"Maybe you can find out what he's up to, Heather," Jenn suggested.

"I plan to try," her friend smiled.

They reached their barn a few minutes later, and Brad helped the girls put the horses in their stalls.

"I know you need to get back to work," Heather said. "If you show us what to do, we can take it from here."

"That would be great," Brad said. "I'll take off their saddles, then I'll show you where their tack goes. Would you mind brushing them a little?"

"Not at all," Heather said.

"Uh, before we do that," Jenn hesitated, "is there a bathroom I can use?"

"Sure thing. It's next to the office. I'll take you there when I go back. We can see how Tiffany's doing, too."

"Do you think she'll be okay?" Jenn asked nervously.

"I think so," Brad replied. "She's had worse spills than that."

Fifteen minutes later Heather found herself crooning to Solar Wind as she groomed the horse's magnificent black coat. She was startled nearly to death, though, when a man asked, "Beautiful, isn't she?"

Heather wheeled around and saw Jon Kent standing there. "Oh, hi," she said breathlessly. "You scared me."

"Sorry," he smiled as he moved closer. "I just happened to walk by and saw you here by yourself." He patted Solar Wind's neck, and the horse nickered. "Did you know that she was one of Rick Spencer's first show horses?"

"No," Heather admitted, surprised. "How old is she?"

"Twenty," he said, yawning. "Please excuse me."

"Sure. How old do horses get?"

"They can live to be forty if they're cared for properly." Jon emphasized the word *if*.

"How old is Arabian Knight?" Heather asked on a hunch.

"Only six. What a shame, his getting colic now."

"Do you think it's a result of someone's negligence, or a deliberate attempt to knock him out of the competition?" she asked boldly.

Jon stared at her. "I really don't know, Heather. I hear you're pretty good at solving mysteries, though."

"Who told you?" Heather tried to sound casual.

"Tiffany. She's real excited about your being here."

"How's her hand?" the teenage sleuth inquired.

"Much better. I think she'll be okay."

In the silence that followed, Heather continued brushing Solar Wind. She felt uncomfortable when the trainer just stood there silently.

"Heather," he finally said, "I could use your help."

The teenager's heart pounded. "You could?"

"Yes. Rick's so-called accident and Arabian Knight's illness have sent this place into a tizzy. That's no good, especially not before the Olympic trials."

"Why do you say, 'Rick's so-called accident'?" she narrowed her hazel eyes.

Jon looked over his shoulder to make sure no one was listening. "Everyone knows that Rick and I have argued over how to run this place. Still, I've given in because he's the owner's son, and I've always respected him—at least, I used to." He inhaled deeply. "I have a hunch that Rick may be disabling the horses."

Heather was surprised. "Why do you think he would do that?"

"I don't know for sure. He's been acting pretty strangely, though, moody and obsessive. I just wonder if you'd keep an eye out for any clues while you're here." Jon put a hand on her right shoulder. "I'd really appreciate it."

Heather looked into his clear blue eyes and melted a bit. *He is handsome,* she thought. Before she could respond, though, Jenn bounced into the barn with her aunt in tow.

"Oh, hi, Jon," Mrs. Blake said. "What's up?"

"I was walking by and stopped to chat with Heather," he said lightly. "I wanted to see whether she and Jenn enjoyed their ride."

"We did," they said together.

"Then you're having a good time," he concluded, pleased. "I'll see you later, then." With a wink in Heather's direction, Jon left.

While the three women finished grooming the horses, Heather thought about what Jon had said. *Based on what Jon and Kim have told me, it sure seems as if Rick Spencer is up to no good,* she concluded.

Heather, Jenn, Tiffany, Brad, and Mrs. Blake got back to San Clemente at two o'clock. On the way home, Tiffany said that her hand felt better and that she didn't want to go for an x-ray. Jenn was still suffering from jet lag and decided to take a nap when they got to the Blake residence.

"I'll join you," Heather said. "I'm pretty sore from my fall this morning."

"I can't believe you got up so early," Jenn shook her head. "Where do you get your energy?"

An hour-long rest and a wonderful dinner of barbecued spare ribs refreshed both teenagers as they ate outside with the Blakes. For dessert Jenn's aunt brought a cherry cobbler out to the patio. Just as they dug in, a flower truck pulled up in front of the house. A young man got out bearing a long, white box.

"Is there a Heather Reed here?" he asked.

"Yes," she answered, totally surprised.

"These are for you."

"Imagine that!" Jenn exclaimed.

Heather took the package, and the delivery man drove away. Heather noticed that the side of the truck read "Mission Florists, San Juan Capistrano."

"They must be from Evan," Jenn teased.

"Who's that?" asked her Uncle Roger.

"The boy she dates back home."

But Evan hadn't sent the long-stemmed red roses. All the color drained from Heather's face as she read the enclosed card: "Think how good these will look on your grave. If you disagree, quit snooping!"

9

First Warning

"Heather, you look like you've seen a ghost!" Mrs. Blake exclaimed. "What's wrong?"

Before Heather could cover up the nasty message, Mr. Blake yanked it from the box. He gave her a searching look. "Why would someone send you this?" he asked as the others jostled to see what it said.

"I-I don't know exactly," she stammered.

"This is downright hateful!" Mrs. Blake exclaimed.

"What have you been 'snooping' about?" Mr. Blake asked.

Heather remembered her promise to Kim Rosen not to say anything about Kim's suspicions. *Then again, I don't know how honest she's being with me,* Heather thought. *I'm beginning to have my doubts about Rick, especially after what both Kim and Jon said. Maybe Kim really is trying to set me up.*

"Heather?" Mr. Blake interrupted her reflections.

The sixteen-year-old decided to share a little of her new mystery, but not all of it. At least not yet.

"You know all that's been going on at Spencer Wood Farm?" she asked. Roger Blake nodded. "Well, I'm really interested in finding out what's behind it. When I was over there today, I must have asked too many questions."

"I didn't think you did anything unusual," Mrs. Blake defended, struggling to remember what Heather might have done to create such a response. "Who did you talk to anyway?"

"I met most of the people who work there," she said innocently. "And Jon Kent asked if I would keep an eye on things. I guess Tiffany told him about my being an amateur detective."

"I did," Tiffany replied nervously. "I hope that was okay."

"That was fine," Heather reassured her. "I'm wondering, though, if anyone overheard Jon and me talking."

Tiffany snorted in disgust. "You know, I wouldn't put anything past Melanie Cutler. She's been acting so hateful. She may be angry enough to do something like this."

"That's a very serious thing to do, though, Tiffany," her father pointed out. "And why would she threaten Heather? It's you she's upset with."

"Unless she's sabotaging the horses," Tiffany argued. Suddenly she relented. "Still, why would she hurt her own horse?"

"This is terribly complicated," Mrs. Blake sighed. "I don't know how you figure out your mysteries, Heather. It must be a gift."

Before Heather could say anything, Mr. Blake became

very angry. "Something weird is going on over there, all right," he stormed. "Tiffany, I have a good notion to pull you out of this competition before anything else happens. You, too, Brad. I don't like the way they've been treating you there. I won't have my children accused of sabotage, or have a guest in my house threatened." He stared at his two children.

"Please don't, Daddy!" Tiffany pleaded tearfully. "Not when I'm this close to the Olympics. Please."

"Are the Olympics more important than your life?" he asked pointedly.

Heather and Jenn felt uncomfortable and remained quiet as Brad and Tiffany pleaded with their dad to let them see the competition through.

Heather took the time to make a mental list of possible suspects. *There are the principals, like Rick and Kim, Jon, and Melanie,* she thought. *Then there's that guy who lives on the property, and the people who are in daily contact with the horses.*

But Heather had no idea what their motives would be. *It doesn't make sense that Melanie or Jon would hurt the horses,* she reasoned, *not when there's so much glory at stake. Then again, why would Rick try to damage his farm's reputation?*

Mr. Blake finally gave in, but the thrill of victory didn't overcome the agony of uncertainty and danger. No one could eat any more. They cleared the table in silence. After Mr. Blake took the roses and the card from Heather, she and Jenn retreated to their room.

"I wonder who sent those flowers?" Jenn asked, stretching out on the bed.

"I'm going to try to find out," Heather said, sitting on the rocking chair. She had stuffed the envelope from the threatening card into her pocket and now retrieved it. "Mission Florists," she read aloud. "Want to come with me to Tiffany's room while I use her phone to call the florist?"

Jenn hopped to her feet. "Sure, but won't Uncle Roger look into that?"

"No doubt, but I want to do some of my own checking."

They went across the hall, and Heather explained her mission to Tiffany.

"Be my guest," the girl said.

The teenage sleuth found the number in the phone book and placed the call. The man who answered said he was just closing for the day, but Heather explained what she wanted, begging him to help her.

"Did someone phone in that order, or come into your store?" she asked.

"Came in," he said shortly, displeased by the delay.

"Were you there?" Her pulse raced.

"Yeah. In fact, I took the order. A young woman, oh, about twenty-two, placed it."

"What was her name?"

"I don't know," the shopkeeper replied. "She paid cash."

"Well, then, what did she look like?" Heather tried.

"Like I said, she was about twenty-two, had dark brown hair, and she wasn't too happy."

"How long was her hair?" the teenager pried as Jenn and Tiffany listened.

"I couldn't tell. She wore it in a ponytail," he said.

"With a scrunchie?" Heather asked eagerly.

"A what?" He grew even more impatient.

"A piece of material that twists over the ponytail."

"I don't know."

"Did you notice what kind of car she drove?" There was a brief pause, and Heather began fearing that he had hung up. "Hello?" she said. "Are you still there?"

"Yes, I'm here," he huffed. "She wasn't driving. I remember seeing her in a blue car. Some old guy with long hair was driving. It would be tough to miss that character. Now, if you'll excuse me, I'm ready to leave."

"Of course," Heather yielded. "Thank you so much!" She was excited, remembering that it had been a blue car that had hit her on the bike.

"Looks like you found out something important," Jenn coaxed.

Heather repeated the conversation to her friends.

"The driver sounds like Cal Mahoney," Tiffany pointed out nervously.

"That's who I thought of, too," Heather agreed.

"Who's that?" Jenn was confused.

"The blacksmith," Tiffany reminded her.

"Oh, yeah. He's the strange one, right?"

Her cousin nodded.

"Tiffany, do you have a dictionary handy?" Heather asked out of the blue.

"A dictionary? Sure. Why?" She got up from her bed and yanked the volume from her desk, a confused look on her face.

"Cal Mahoney has an odd license plate," Heather explained. "It says 'DANSE,' and I want to know what that means." She began flipping through the pages to the "D" section. "Hmm," she reflected. "It says to check *Dance of Death.*"

"Sounds horrid," Jenn shivered.

"What does it say?" Tiffany prodded.

"It says the expression is also known as the *Danse Macabre,* and it's from Medieval art. Artists used to paint scenes in which Death led people to their graves."

"That rings a bell," Tiffany commented. "In school last year we talked about how art from that period got into death because so many people died in plagues." She paused, then added, "You know, I once heard Cal say that he had lived back in the Middle Ages. Ridiculous, isn't it?"

"I think so, but many people are misled into believing that stuff," Heather remarked. "He seems dangerous, and I think we'd better keep an eye on him."

"So, do you think the guy driving this woman to the florist was Cal?" Jenn asked.

"I think that's a good possibility," Heather told her.

"What about the woman?" Tiffany asked.

"I'm wondering whether her description fits anyone you know."

Tiffany thought for a moment. "There's one possibility," she frowned deeply. "It sounds a little like Debra Easley. And that girl is trouble."

10

Ghost Story

Heather leaned closer. "What do you mean?"

"Debra's a few years older than me," Tiffany began. "She just graduated from college. Her parents own Bar None Farm just south of here."

"Is she competing for an Olympic spot, too?" Jenn asked.

"Not that I know," her cousin replied. "It's funny, but the last time I talked to her, Debra said she was planning to become a journalist. Now I hear that she's running Bar None."

"Why did you say she's trouble?" Heather followed up.

"Her riders say she's mean and nasty," Tiffany explained.

"And she hadn't been before?"

"Debra's always been a little quiet, but not mean."

"Sounds like something's wrong in her life," Heather pondered.

"You know, I've heard rumors that Bar None's horses

have been more injury and illness-prone than usual. I wonder if that has anything to do with us?"

"Maybe there's a conspiracy," Jenn suggested dramatically.

Her cousin stared at Jenn. "That's awful!"

Heather agreed. "Awful, but believable."

"It makes me sick that anyone would hurt an innocent, trusting horse," Tiffany said angrily. "They depend on us for everything. It's not right. It also isn't right that someone would threaten you, Heather."

"Thanks, but right now I'm more concerned for the horses," Heather responded. "At least I can take care of myself."

As Heather finished brushing her teeth that night, Jenn became serious. "I know something's going on. Can you tell me about it?"

Heather wished she could discuss her meeting with Kim Rosen, but that was a secret. "I'm starting to figure something out," she said, side-stepping the issue. "You saw how spiteful Melanie Cutler was toward Tiffany today."

"Oh, I know! That was awful," Jenn responded.

"There's quite a rivalry going on there."

"But Tiffany wouldn't have made her own horse sick, would she?" Jenn asked in disbelief.

"Probably not," Heather said slowly. "But let's not forget, there's another Olympic hopeful at Spencer Wood Farm."

"That Dean Parmi guy," Jenn nodded.

"Right, and apparently he's not exactly sweetness and light either."

"So, we should watch him, too?" the redhead guessed.

"Exactly."

"I guess the staff also should be watched?"

"I think so," Heather nodded grimly.

Suddenly Jenn snapped her fingers. "I wonder if that girl who got dismissed could tell you anything."

"Abby," Heather repeated. "I've been thinking about her, too. I think she may be taking a fall for someone else."

"Exactly," Jenn nodded.

"I want to meet her. Maybe we can tomorrow."

"But how?" Jenn asked.

"I'm not sure yet."

"Aren't you scared, Heather? That note with the flowers and the *danse* thing gave me the creeps."

"A little," she admitted. "Like I said, though, I'm more afraid for those beautiful horses. Besides, I'll be careful."

"And I'll probably end up bound and gagged," Jenn sighed.

Early the following morning Mrs. Blake told her guests that she was going to her job as a doctor's receptionist. "I'd been hoping for the week off, but my back-up has the flu," she explained. "That means you girls will need to spend the day at the farm or hang around here. The

Volkswagen still isn't working, so Brad and Tiffany will drop me off on their way to Spencer Wood."

Yes! Heather thought excitedly. *A whole day to investigate!*

After Tiffany dropped her mother off forty-five minutes later, she, Brad, Jenn, and Heather drove to the farm.

"I'm so glad your hand feels better today," Jenn told Tiffany.

"Me, too!" her cousin exclaimed.

"Would you mind if Jenn and I went exploring after we watch you train?" Heather asked her.

Tiffany's eyes narrowed. "Exploring? What do you mean?"

"I'd like to meet Abby Valeet," Heather confessed.

"What about that threat?"

"I won't let that stop me," she answered. "Would you tell me where Abby lives?"

Brad and his sister looked at each other for guidance, wondering whether they should tell Heather. Finally Tiffany decided to go along with her—for now. "How about if I drop you off, then show you how to get back to the farm?" she suggested. "The Valeets only live a mile away."

"All right, but it is pretty early," Heather noted.

"Abby's an early riser," Brad stated.

"By the way, I heard that your vet lives about two miles from the farm," Heather suddenly remembered.

"She and Abby are practically neighbors," Tiffany said.

Jenn's mind was elsewhere. "How will we get inside Spencer Wood when we're finished?" she asked. "Remember that guard?"

"I'll just tell him that you and Heather wanted to go for a walk, so we dropped you off before we got there," Brad stated.

"I think that's reasonable," Jenn nodded.

Several minutes later, they pulled in front of a sprawling ranch house graced by dozens of potted flowers.

"It looks cheerful," said Jenn.

"And there's Abby!" Tiffany exclaimed.

A pleasant-looking young woman looked up from weeding a flower bed. Noticing her friends, she ran to the station wagon.

"Tiffany! Brad!" she called out.

"Hi, Abby!" they said from the car.

"Have you come to visit?" Her brown eyes glowed with delight.

"Tiff and I are on our way to the farm," Brad said. "But this is my cousin, Jenn, and her friend Heather. They're visiting from Philadelphia and wanted to meet you."

"Meet me?" she pointed to herself.

"Heather is really good at solving mysteries," Tiffany broke in. "She'd like to ask you some questions. Will you help her?"

"Oh, sure!" Abby said, pulling Heather's sleeve as she got out of the car.

Brad and Tiffany drove away, and Abby led the girls

to wrought iron chairs under a shade tree. "What do you want to know?" she asked eagerly.

"What happened Saturday?" Heather began.

"Don't you know?" Abby asked innocently.

"We've heard the story," Jenn smiled, "but we want to hear your version."

"Well," she said eagerly, "I helped Brad clean the stalls. That took nearly all day. We did a good job."

"I'm sure," Heather grinned. "Were you there all day?"

"I ate supper here, then went back." Looking embarrassed, she lowered her voice and said, "I fell asleep."

"In the barn?" the sleuth continued.

"Yes," Abby said. "I was in the office. I fell asleep in the chair. I do that sometimes. No one ever minded before."

"Were you alone?"

"When I woke up, I was," Abby stated.

"Then what happened?"

"I saw a ghost!" she shuddered. "It had long hair that glowed. It was on a horse."

"Where did you see it?" Heather questioned.

"At the entrance to the barn. It hissed at me like this," she said, making a sharp noise. "I heard one of the dogs barking, too."

"Was it a male or a female?"

"I don't know," she sputtered. "It was a dog."

"No," Heather smiled, "I mean the ghost?"

"I don't know," Abby repeated, puzzled.

"What kind of horse did it ride?"

"Black. The other horses all started neighing."

"What did you do?" Jenn broke in.

"I screamed and ran all the way home." She hung her head sadly. "Tori Caine won't let me go back. She thinks I hurt Arabian Knight. I think the ghost did it, though," Abby said confidentially.

Heather pulled the ponytail scrunchie out of her shorts pocket and showed it to Abby. "Is this yours?"

The girl merely glanced at it. "No, but it sure is pretty." Abby became distracted. "Do you like my flowers?"

Heather put the hair ornament back. "I think they're beautiful." To get her back on track Heather asked, "On Saturday did anything else strange happen at the farm, Abby?"

She thought hard but couldn't remember anything. Heather had another idea. "Was there anyone around who usually isn't?"

"You mean like a visitor?" Abby asked.

"Yes, it could have been a visitor."

The young woman began naming everyone she had seen at the farm that day. Heather suddenly interrupted her. "Did you say Debra Easley?"

"Yeah," Abby said in disgust.

"You don't like her?" Jenn asked.

"No! She's mean. I don't know why she comes around."

Heather and Jenn exchanged glances, wondering what this could mean. Just then a tall, irate woman ran toward them wielding a garden hoe and yelling, "Get out of here if you know what's good for you!"

11

Horsing Around

Marie!" Abby exclaimed, jumping up. "These are my new friends, Jenn and Heather. They're all right."

"Are they from that farm?" Marie demanded as the teenagers' hearts raced.

"No," Abby said. "Jenn's cousin trains there, though."

The woman put down the hoe. "I told you not to associate with those people after what they did to you."

"This is my big sister, Marie," Abby said proudly.

Heather and Jenn simply nodded. Neither could muster a greeting after the way Marie Valeet had "welcomed" them.

"What are you doing here?" the woman put her hands on her hips.

Abby spared them the effort of replying. "They're asking about the ghost."

"Why?" Marie's dark brown eyes narrowed.

"I think it's wrong that Abby got fired," Heather stammered. "I'm hoping to clear her so she can get her job back."

"Don't do her any favors," Marie rumbled.

"Oh, I want to go back!" Abby wailed. "Please, Marie."

"We'll talk about that later. You're just upsetting her," the woman told her sister's guests curtly. Then she yanked Abby by the hand and led her back to the house. "Don't come back unless you're invited," she called over her shoulder.

As Heather and Jenn walked to the road, the redhead whispered, "She's about as friendly as a pit bull!" Her friend grinned. "I bet Rick Spencer wouldn't have let Abby go," Jenn said after a brief pause. But Heather still wasn't sure about his role in the mystery. "By the way, I wonder how he's doing."

"Hopefully we'll find out when we get to the farm."

When they arrived, the guard opened the gate to let them enter. Just then, a snarling dog leaped toward them.

"Get him away!" Jenn screamed. Panic-stricken, she ran as fast as she could. The dog went after her.

"Sit!" Heather commanded.

The hefty young guard lunged after the dog as it paused, but the animal turned from Jenn and snapped at him. A man wearing a carpenter's apron came running to help. Heather watched as the guard raised his pistol. He couldn't bring himself to shoot the dog, though.

"Hurry, Heather!" Jenn cried out.

"Go on!" the guard urged. "We've got his attention now."

Tori Caine ran in from the practice field. "What is going on here?" she demanded.

"That, that dog attacked Heather and me," Jenn stammered.

"Well, c'mon. Let's get you two to the barn while they calm it down." Tori yelled toward the guard and the carpenter. "Hurry up! He's upsetting the horses!"

"Who's dog is that?" Heather asked as they hurried along.

"Probably some stray," she said. "It isn't one of ours, that's for sure. It's just what this place needs right now."

"What's wrong?" asked a woman who had just popped out of a large van parked near the main barn. Heather recognized her as Dr. Sandies, the veterinarian.

Tori explained the situation to the doctor, who clucked her tongue. "Is the situation under control now?" she asked.

"I think so," Tori said. "I'd better get back to the field. You know how Jon gets if I'm not at his beck and call." The weary manager rolled her eyes and left.

"Perhaps I'd better check on the dog," Dr. Sandies told the teenagers.

"Good luck," Jenn muttered.

"I'd like to go along if you don't mind, Dr. Sandies," Heather said. Jenn looked at her friend as if she'd lost it.

The vet regarded her oddly. "Whatever for, child?"

"I'd like to see what happens," she said casually.

"Well, all right," Dr. Sandies consented.

The dog was still snapping at the guard and the carpenter when they arrived. Heather stayed far away from the canine as she watched Dr. Sandies speak soothingly to it. *The dog is quieting down for Dr. Sandies,* Heather noticed. *It seems to know her voice.*

"Are you going to tranquilize it?" asked the guard.

"I don't think I need to," Dr. Sandies smiled charmingly. "I'll take it to my van and see that it gets to the pound."

"Weird place," Heather heard the guard tell the carpenter.

Dr. Sandies led the dog past the teenager, and it growled. "Stop that!" the vet ordered, and it did.

That really is odd, Heather reflected. *I wonder if she put the dog up to attacking me and Jenn. Why would a vet do such a thing, though?*

The teenage sleuth took her troubled thoughts and walked back to the guard. "I heard you say something a minute ago about this being a strange place."

The man shook his head. "Between what's going on with the horses and people coming and going at all hours, it's enough to drive a person crazy."

Heather frowned. "What do you mean, 'people coming and going at all hours?'"

"These people really train hard, you know," he said.

I wonder what that's about, she thought.

"My buddy's on duty at night, and he said there's riders out there after midnight," the guard explained.

Heather became excited. "Does he know who?"

The guard shrugged. "Mostly Mr. Kent. Then that blacksmith hangs around, too."

"When was the last time that happened?"

"I don't know about last night," he remarked, "but they were out there the night before."

"Doing what?"

"Mr. Kent was in the practice field," the guard told her.

"My buddy said he didn't know what the other dude was up to."

Heather thanked him and hurried back to the main barn, her thoughts in a whirl. On the way she spotted Dean Parmi on his horse and tried to get his attention. She had questions she wanted to ask him.

"Excuse me," she called out. "Dean!"

"Quit bugging me," he answered rudely and galloped away.

What a guy! she thought. Back in the barn she saw that Dr. Sandies was with a restless Arabian Knight. Melanie Cutler stood nearby biting her nails.

"Do you have to take him to the hospital?" the rider asked.

"I'm afraid so," the vet concluded. "The colic has worsened. He's a very sick horse."

Melanie rested her head against Arabian Knight's neck and cried softly. Heather almost felt sorry for her—until Melanie yelled at her.

"What are you looking at? Isn't this the break your dear friend Tiffany wanted?"

"No," Heather said evenly, "it isn't."

"Girls," the vet said, turning to Heather and Jenn, "would you please get Melanie some tissues from the office?"

They nodded and went across the hall. Heather found the tissues on the walnut desk, and, picking them up, she noticed a crumpled scrap of paper lying next to the trash can. It seemed out of place in the immaculate room, and she bent over to pick it up. Heather was about to toss it into the garbage when the word *danse* caught her eye. Unfolding it she read, "Let's Danse Thursday midnight." She quickly stuffed the paper in her pocket with trembling hands. *I've got to tell Jenn about this,* Heather decided.

A few minutes later, she suggested that they go for a ride. "Sure!" Jenn agreed. "I loved it yesterday."

They went to the barn and asked permission to take out Solar Wind and Master Mind. Brad helped them outfit the horses, then the teenagers went to a field near the Spencer mansion. Solar Wind seemed a bit fidgety, but under control. Once Heather was far away from prying eyes, she told Jenn what the guard had said. Then she showed her the strange note.

"That's really weird," the redhead asserted.

"Jenn, I have a feeling something bad may happen tonight."

"Like what?" she asked, her blue eyes wide.

"I'm afraid that Cal Mahoney may try to kill a horse."

"How awful!" Jenn exclaimed. "What're you going to do?"

"First, let's visit that man who lives in the trailer," she said resolutely.

"Why?"

"I want to know what he's all about. He may know what's going on."

"But he may hurt you," Jenn protested.

"That's a chance I'll have to take," Heather remarked. "Those horses need my—"

Before she could finish, Solar Wind suddenly reared up. Heather fell backward as Jenn screamed.

12

Night Rider

Heather, are you all right?" her friend cried out.

The petite teenager shook her head back and forth a few times as Solar Wind stood nearby gazing at her. "I'm okay," Heather answered, "just a bit jolted." She got up and mounted the horse.

"Do you think you should do that?" Jenn fretted.

"You know what they say about falling off a horse," she grinned. "She seems okay," Heather said, stroking Solar Wind's glossy black neck. "I think she just got spooked."

"Speaking of which," Jenn said dryly, "I am, too. Let's go back, Heather. Why do you want to talk to that guy anyway?"

"It's so odd that no one seems to know what he's doing here. I wonder if even Mrs. Spencer knows."

They were about to find out. As Heather and Jenn poked around the silver trailer on horseback, a woman in her fifties and an older man startled them.

"Who are you, and what do you want?" she asked sharply.

"We, uh, were wondering whether Mr., uh, Mr.—the man who lives here is home," Heather faltered.

"I believe the name you want is Doston," the man supplied.

"We were wondering if he might talk to us," she said.

"And who might you be?" Although the woman's eyes couldn't be seen behind her sunglasses, Heather imagined they were narrowed. She also thought this might be Mrs. Spencer because of a gold monogram pin on her red blouse that read "MGS."

"I'm Heather Reed, and this is Jenn McLaughlin. Jenn is Tiffany Blake's cousin."

"What do you want with me?" the man asked suspiciously.

"Are you Mr. Doston?" Heather asked.

"I am, and this is Mrs. Spencer," he eyed Heather critically.

"We saw Rick the other day at the hospital," Jenn said nervously. "How is he?"

That reminded Heather of something else. *I haven't heard from Kim either,* she thought. *I wonder what's what with her.* "He's improving nicely," Mrs. Spencer said, interrupting Heather's reflections. Still, she looked upset. "I think it's time for you to go," she concluded firmly.

"Wait a minute, Margaret." Her companion held up his right hand and faced Heather. "What's so important that you want to talk to an old man?" Something in Jenn's tone as she asked about Rick had convinced Mr. Doston that the girls were sincere.

"I've heard that someone's been riding in the practice field at night," Heather began as Solar Wind tossed her head impatiently. The teenager loosened the reigns and let the horse eat grass. "I wonder if you've seen him?" Heather asked.

Both Mrs. Spencer and Mr. Doston were amazed. "How did you know?" the woman gasped.

"The guard told me about it," Heather responded.

"Mr. Doston was just telling me about the night rider," she told the teenagers.

"So, you've seen the person, too, Mr. Doston?" Heather questioned. The elderly man nodded. "Was it Jon Kent?" she continued.

"Uh-huh," he said.

"Have you also seen the blacksmith?" she inquired.

"Yes," Mr. Doston answered. "In fact, the other night he put on a white sheet and scared that young woman in the stable."

"So, that was Abby's ghost!" Jenn exclaimed.

"I was poking around, trying to figure out what Jon Kent was up to when I saw the so-called phantom," Mr. Doston went on. "I figured it was someone's idea of a joke. When I heard the girl had been let go, though, I decided to tell Margaret about it."

"I'll have to speak with Jon," Mrs. Spencer remarked.

"I wonder if you'd let me try a different approach," the teenage detective suggested. Heather quickly explained that she was good at solving mysteries and had been looking into the problems at the farm.

Mrs. Spencer was skeptical. "What do you have in mind?"

"I'd like to watch him at night from a safe distance. If you confront Jon, he can always deny what's going on or make something up."

"Or he could do something worse to the horses," Jenn said darkly.

"I think it's a good idea," Mr. Doston approved.

Margaret Spencer sighed. "I wish Rick could handle this."

"I'll do whatever I can to help," Doston reassured her. "I owe you and your husband so much."

"You know," Jenn said, "we've been wondering about you. No one seems to know what you're doing here."

"Mr. Doston was my husband's top jockey years ago when we had race horses," Mrs. Spencer explained. She, too, believed the girls were trying to be helpful.

"When I fell on hard times a while back, the Spencers agreed to let me live here in the trailer," Doston continued. "Unfortunately, Mr. Spencer had his stroke and never got to tell anyone about me, so all sorts of rumors got spread around."

Mrs. Spencer looked upset with herself. "I've been too preoccupied to put those stories to rest. I am sorry, Walter."

Heather felt good about the explanation. "I'll try to come by tonight and check out the situation," she said. "I'd feel better if you would help, Mr. Doston. Would you?"

He readily consented. "Of course."

"How will you get past the guard, Heather?" Jenn asked.

"Don't worry. I'll speak to him," Mrs. Spencer said.

"Ah, Mrs. Spencer!" someone called out.

Turning around, they saw Dr. Sandies walking toward them. "I haven't seen you in ages," the vet said. "Hello, girls."

"Hello," they said politely, but Heather thought the vet seemed chilly toward them.

Mrs. Spencer looked a bit guilty. "How are you?"

"Fine, just fine." She nodded toward Doston as if she expected to be introduced. When that didn't happen, Dr. Sandies told them, "Jon and I agree that Arabian Knight should be taken to my clinic. It's such a shame that the horse isn't getting better." She shook her head sadly. "I'll do it after Melanie Cutler leaves for the day so she won't be quite so upset."

"Do what you must," Mrs. Spencer said impatiently. "As you know, I've left matters in my son's hands."

"Yes, I know. It's too bad about him, too. How is he?"

"About the same," the dignified Mrs. Spencer replied.

"You've had so much trouble lately," Dr. Sandies commented.

"Well, that's about to end," Margaret Spencer showed some spirit. "Jon Kent and the blacksmith have been hanging around at night scaring people, and Heather's going to help my friend here figure out what's going on."

Heather's eyes nearly popped out in disbelief. *That might ruin everything!* she groaned to herself as Jenn shot her an astonished look.

"I think it's time we said good-bye," Mr. Doston said quickly, trying to salvage the situation.

Mrs. Spencer caught on. "Yes, well, it was good seeing you again, Dr. Sandies. Girls." She nodded and walked away.

"I hope she didn't blow it," Heather said miserably when she was alone with Jenn several minutes later.

"Uh, Heather, yesterday morning you didn't really go fishing, did you?" Jenn asked searchingly as they rode over to the practice field where Tiffany was jumping.

"Yes, I did."

"But you didn't go to the pier just for fishing, right?"

Heather faced her best friend squarely. "Jenn, I'd love to tell you all about it, but right now, I can't. Trust me?"

"Sure," Jenn said glumly. "I just wish I knew."

"I'll tell you when I can," Heather promised.

On the ride home from the farm that afternoon, Brad had more bad news. Tori Caine had warned him that he was going to be fired if anything else happened to the horses. "She found Meridian's hay net mounted too low to the ground," Brad explained. "If a net is set improperly, a horse can get its legs tangled in the bracket, and that's bad news. Dean Parmi had a fit and demanded that Tori reprimand me."

"Brad didn't do it," Tiffany charged. "He would never make such a stupid mistake."

"That must be really upsetting," Heather commented.

"It is!" Brad exclaimed. "Those poor horses."

"Who's responsible for the hay net?" she probed.

"I took care of it, and everything was fine."

"So, someone did it on purpose," Jenn guessed.

"It sure seems that way," Heather announced. "Was anyone suspicious hanging around?"

"Everyone seems suspicious right now," Tiffany frowned. "As usual, Melanie got nasty about it and accused Brad of conspiring against her and Dean so I'll have the best shot at the Olympics. Then Dean turned around and accused me of being against him. I'm getting so sick of this!" Her hands stiffened on the wheel.

"How dare they!" Jenn hollered.

"I haven't really met Dean," Heather said. "I've tried to say hello, but he walks right past me."

"He's royalty, don't you know?" Tiffany asked sarcastically. She paused then said, "You know, what worries me the most is that something might happen to Surfer Girl. If someone's hurting the other horses, why not mine, too? She's already a little wild."

I hope to prevent anything worse from happening, Heather determined.

When the teenagers picked Mrs. Blake up at work, they told her all that had happened at the farm. She was understandably upset and vowed to have a talk with Tori Caine and Jon Kent. Then she announced that she was too tired to cook. "Let's eat out tonight," she suggested. "I think we could all use a pick-me-up."

"Will Dad meet us somewhere?" Brad asked.

"No. He's working late again."

"How about going Mexican?" Jenn asked. "I've been dying to try some real tacos and enchiladas."

"Gosh, I was thinking of spaghetti," Brad said.

"I know!" Mrs. Blake smiled. "Let's go to Qué Pasta, the Italian-Mexican place."

"Perfect," Tiffany approved.

The eastern girls enjoyed the meal so much that they

over-ate. Afterward, as they all waddled through the Blake's front door, Jenn said, "I think I need a nap."

"I'd like to go bike-riding," Tiffany stated. "I need to burn off some calories."

"I'm going to my computer," Brad said. "See you later."

"I'll go riding with you, Tiffany," Heather offered. She thought it might clear her mind. *It's all crammed with questions,* she thought. *Like why hasn't Kim called back? When will I hear from Katarina? And why hasn't Jon Kent talked to me alone since he first asked me to keep an eye on Rick?*

They went to the garage, and Heather told Tiffany what had happened the previous day with Brad's bike.

"Are you over the soreness?" she asked, concerned.

"I'm a little stiff yet, but I'd still like to go with you."

Just as the teenagers were about to leave, however, Brad called to Heather from the balcony of his room.

"I have something to show you on the computer," he said.

"Can't it wait?" Tiffany asked impatiently.

"I don't think so."

"That's okay," Heather said, eager to find out what was going on. *Maybe another clue?* she thought.

Heather raced upstairs to the computer in the family room. The sun's final rays made a last stand on the sofa.

"What's up?" she asked, leaning over Brad's shoulder.

"It's really weird, but there's an urgent message addressed to you on my e-mail," he answered.

Leaning closer, Heather read, "I need your help. Fast! 555-6201. K.R."

13

Truth or Consequences

"Heather? Heather?" Brad called.

The sixteen-year-old snapped out of her deep concentration. "Sorry. I need to use a phone."

"There's one in my parents' room."

Heather raced across the hall and quickly placed the call. Kim Rosen answered on the first ring.

"Heather!" she breathed. "I was afraid you'd never call."

"Where are you, Kim?" she asked.

"My apartment, and I'm terrified," Kim spoke rapidly. "You simply must come. I've got to talk to you."

Heather wondered how in the world she could see Kim without anyone knowing. *That's impossible,* she decided. *I'll try another approach.*

"Heather, are you there?" Kim asked anxiously.

"I'm here," came the response. "I was trying to figure out how to get there when I don't have a car."

"I'd come and get you, but I'm afraid to leave the apartment," Kim's voice trembled. "Please come."

"I think I can swing it, but there's just one catch."

"What's that?"

Heather explained, "I either have to ask Mrs. Blake's permission or get Tiffany and Brad to bring me to your place."

"I can't let anyone know what's happening!" Kim wailed.

"That's the only way I can help you," Heather remained steadfast. *I'm not even sure I can trust her,* she thought. *Not after that hit-and-run episode anyway.* She heard a clicking sound on the line.

"Excuse me," Kim said suddenly. "I have call waiting, and someone's trying to reach me. Please don't go."

"I won't," Heather promised.

The frenzied young woman returned seconds later. "It's happened again!" she cried out. "Someone keeps calling me and not saying anything."

"Have you reported it?" Heather asked.

"No!" Kim panicked. "I can't, remember? Especially not now."

"What's going on, Kim?" Heather asked, wondering whether she was setting up a trap or was genuinely in danger.

"I'm afraid to tell you on the phone. Listen, if you must bring Brad and Tiffany, it's okay with me. Just come. Tiffany knows where I live."

Heather hung up and said a quick prayer that she would do the right thing. Then she returned to Brad.

"Is everything all right?" he asked, concerned.

"Not really. The message was from Kim Rosen, and

she's scared to death. She begged me to come over," Heather explained.

"I didn't know that you were friends with her."

"I'm not exactly," Heather stated. "I think if you go, it will become clearer."

"I have an idea," he answered, thinking quickly.

Brad got out of his e-mail program and turned off the computer. Then he and Heather went into the living room where his mother, Tiffany, and Jenn were watching home videos.

"I hate to break this up," Brad announced, "but Heather and I are in the mood for a ride. We want you to go, too," he said, looking at Jenn and his sister.

Although the two girls were surprised, both thought it was a great idea.

"How about Mom?" Tiffany questioned.

"I think Mom's going to stay right here," Mrs. Blake laughed. "I want to be here when your dad gets home in an hour. Go, and enjoy yourselves. Just don't get back too late."

"I can't," Tiffany said, "not with my training schedule."

The teenagers climbed into the Blakes' station wagon, and Heather explained what was going on. She was careful not to betray any of Kim's confidences. *She can tell them whatever she wants,* Heather reasoned.

Kim lived in a fashionable section of San Juan Capistrano, near the ocean. *She must come from a wealthy family,* Heather concluded upon seeing Kim's expensive apartment.

"Please sit down," Kim gestured to a couch and chairs in her living room. Her hands were shaking, and Heather began to think this was not a set-up after all. "Forgive me if I don't offer refreshments, but I've got so much on my mind."

"What's going on?" Tiffany asked.

Kim inhaled sharply. "I suppose I can trust all of you. I don't know where else to turn."

With that, the Englishwoman quickly told Tiffany, Brad, and Jenn what really had happened to Rick and how he had been behaving strangely before and after the shooting. They sat in amazement. Heather followed up with an account of her bike "accident" Tuesday morning.

Kim was horrified. "We've got to find out who's behind all this before someone gets killed," she insisted.

"It sounds like this is a case of sabotage." Brad stated.

"I didn't know the situation was this bad," Tiffany said gravely.

"It is," Kim nodded. Then she told them, "I keep getting strange calls. Someone rings me up but doesn't say anything. It's got me frantic because the person who shot Rick is still at large."

"Not exactly a comforting thought," Jenn quipped.

"The worse thing is, right before supper I visited Rick in hospital," Kim said in her British way. "And guess what?"

"What?" they all asked.

"He wasn't there!"

"He wasn't there?" Tiffany repeated dumbly.

"What happened?" Heather asked.

"He was released without my knowing!" Kim exclaimed. "I saw him this afternoon, and he never said a word about it to me. I knew Rick was better, but I had no idea he was ready to leave." Kim started crying softly. "Why didn't he tell me?"

Heather had a bad feeling about Rick.

"That is awful," Tiffany stated. "You must be so upset."

"I am," Kim nodded, blowing her nose.

"What do you make of it, Heather?" Jenn asked.

"I think it's serious." She gave Kim a searching look. "Are you telling us everything?"

"Y-yes," she stammered. "Why?"

"It's critical that I have as much information as possible before I do anything else."

"Well, I called Rick at home, and he wasn't there," Kim said. "Is that important?"

"You bet," Heather commented. *You know,* she told herself, *I think Kim's all right. I can't say the same yet for Rick.*

"What do we do now?" Tiffany asked.

Everyone looked to Heather. She told them about the *danse* note and her plan to visit the farm that night to see what Jon and the blacksmith were doing.

"Why in the world is Jon riding at night?" Tiffany asked. "You said the blacksmith comes, too?"

Heather told them about her talk with Walter Doston and Mrs. Spencer. "He even told us that Cal Mahoney was the 'phantom' Abby Valeet saw. I have a hunch that he scared her away so he could tamper with the horses."

Brad became angry. "I'd like to tamper with him!"

"Heather, I don't think you should go there alone tonight," Jenn remarked nervously.

"Do you want to come with me?" Heather teased.

"No!"

"I'll go," Kim announced. "Maybe I can help. Besides, I can drive you there."

"You know, I think that's a good idea," Heather approved.

"There's one slight problem here," Tiffany pointed out. "If Kim drives you to the farm, what are we going to tell Mom and Dad when you're not with us?"

"Hmm, that is a problem," Heather mused. She thought quietly for a moment. "I know! Kim can ask Tiffany, Jenn, and me to stay overnight with her because she's been having nightmares ever since the robbery. She'll see that Tiffany gets to her training session in the morning. Then Tiff and Jenn can stay at Kim's and try to trace the prank caller while Kim and I go to the farm."

Brad laughed. "You think of everything, don't you?"

"I hope so," Heather said seriously.

14

The Fifth Horseman

Permission was given for the girls to stay at Kim's, and Brad returned home.

"So far, so good," Heather announced as she got into Kim's white convertible.

"Yes, but this whole thing gives me the frights," Kim shook her head. After a few minutes she said, "You know, Heather, I feel I owe you one."

"What do you mean?" Heather asked.

"It's because of me that you were run down on that bike."

"What makes you think that?" the teenager asked, suddenly on guard.

"Of course, I don't know for sure," Kim said without a trace of defensiveness. "It just seems strange that you were attacked right after you met with me."

Heather relaxed. *I must be getting paranoid,* she told herself.

After pulling onto the freeway, Kim asked, "Heather, what do you think is going on?"

"Someone is deliberately harming the horses," she

stated. "I'm not sure who, though, or for what reason. It could be to give one of the Olympic hopefuls an edge. There's just one thing that bothers me about that."

"What is it?" Kim inquired.

"All three contenders' horses have been attacked in one way or another."

"So, if one of the competitors was doing this to the horses, why would his or her horse also be affected?" Kim pondered.

"Exactly," Heather said. "Then there's this business with Jon Kent riding at night in the company of that blacksmith. And, of course, how is what happened to Rick related to all of this?"

"I'm glad you're the one trying to figure this out," Kim stated. "It's beyond me, that's for sure."

Suddenly the light dawned on Heather. "Kim!" she shouted.

"What?" she asked urgently.

"I think I have it!"

"Have what?" Kim's voice was tense.

"I heard that Jon Kent didn't quite make the Olympics."

"That's true," Kim nodded. "It's always been a thorn in his side. Even his brilliance as a trainer hasn't erased the pain."

"But Rick went to the Olympics, and he medaled," Heather continued.

"What are you getting at?"

"I wonder, did that accomplishment mean much financially?"

"Not as much as it does for, say, a figure skater or swimmer. In the horse world itself there's a lot of money to be made, though."

"Then Jon missed out on both gold and glory," Heather guessed. "It's just possible, Kim, that he may be trying to knock Tiffany, Melanie, and Dean out of the competition. He may be preparing to make a surprise showing at the Olympic trials. Why else would he be riding at night?"

"That makes sense to me," Kim said. "How does Rick fit in?"

"Maybe he found out what Jon was up to," she suggested.

"If Jon would shoot Rick and injure horses just to make the Olympic team, he must be stopped," Kim said angrily.

"Jon and his accomplices," Heather corrected. "I'm certain he's not in this alone."

When the young women arrived at Spencer Wood Farm, Kim parked a quarter of a mile up the road so no one would recognize her car. They walked to the gate and ran into their first obstacle.

"I don't know what you want at this hour, but no one can come in," the guard growled at them.

"Mrs. Spencer sent word that I'd be coming. My name is Heather Reed," she said evenly.

"Yes, she did say something about you," the middle-aged man consented. "But Mrs. Spencer never mentioned her." He pointed to Kim. "How did you get here anyway?" he asked suspiciously.

"In a car." Heather struggled not to get sarcastic. It was eleven o'clock, and she was anxious to get to Walter Doston's trailer so she could spy on Jon Kent and Cal Mahoney.

"All right," he grumbled, "but you people are pushing it."

"What do you mean?" Heather asked.

"It's been in and out, in and out all night, and everyone has an excuse."

"Who else is here?" Heather questioned. She had a feeling that something was terribly wrong. Kim clutched her sleeve in alarm.

"That crazy blacksmith, Jon Kent, the vet, some girl, and a guy I haven't seen before," the guard stated. "Now, if you please, I want to lock the gate before the next batch arrives."

"What next batch?" Kim asked.

"There's bound to be more," he said.

Heather and Kim hurried up the dirt road to the barns. "I thought you said the note you found mentioned midnight," Kim said urgently.

"I have a feeling they pushed up the time," the teenager said. She explained how Mrs. Spencer had inadvertently told Dr. Sandies about Heather's plan to spy on the night rider.

"There are only two of us and five of them," Kim's voice trembled.

"I wonder who the fifth one is," Heather mused.

As they neared the first out-building where farm equipment was stored, Heather and her companion saw a red sports car. Kim became highly agitated.

"That's it!" she whispered fiercely. "That's the car that the guy who shot Rick was driving!"

"I wonder how it's avoided the police?" Heather asked.

"Oh, Heather, this is awful." Kim gripped her arm tightly. "I hope Rick is all right."

Brad Blake had gone to his computer to check his e-mail messages. The first one caught his eye immediately. *It's a reply from Heather's Austrian friend!* he thought excitedly. *I don't think she'd mind my reading this.* Brad was incredulous as he read the electronic letter. He made a print-out and bounded across the hall to his parents' room.

"Mom, look at this!" Brad said urgently. "Heather got a message from that Austrian girl with the horse farm." Then he told them all that had happened. "Katarina's trainer was arrested for selling injured or previously-ill horses at inflated prices, among them, Arabian Knight, Meridian, and Surfer Girl. Apparently, the buyers insure them for more money than the horses are worth. Then they collect a large sum when the horses die."

"How did they get away with it?" Mr. Blake asked.

"Dr. Sandies checked them out when they came. She should have known."

"I think she did know," Brad sputtered.

"But why?" his mother said helplessly.

"I think we'd better get over to the farm," her husband announced. "I have a hunch that Heather and Kim might be walking right into a trap."

A few minutes later, Mr. Blake jumped into his police cruiser and headed, lights flashing, for Spencer Wood Farm. He radioed for back-up. Brad and his mother picked up Jenn and Tiffany in the station wagon and also headed to the farm.

"I hope we're not too late," Mrs. Blake worried.

"No one's here," Heather said quietly as they entered the big barn.

"But someone has been," Kim pointed to the open door.

Just then something clattered to the ground. "What's that?" she cried out.

Shining her flashlight downward, Heather saw an empty thermos rolling loudly across the floor. "That belongs to Cal Mahoney," the teenage detective said. "His truck isn't here, though. Maybe he came with someone else, like that girl who bought the flowers with the threatening note." Heather quickly told Kim all about that. "Let's see if all the horses are here," she concluded.

Moments later Kim announced, "Arabian Knight is missing!"

Heather wasn't surprised. "I heard Dr. Sandies say she was going to take him to her clinic."

What she discovered next did surprise her, though. "Surfer Girl is gone, too!"

As Kim ran toward Heather, she tripped over something. "Oh, my goodness!" she exclaimed. "It's Mr. Doston!"

15

Reins of Danger

Kim recklessly turned on a light near the office and hovered over the prone figure as Heather checked his vital signs. "Is he alive?" the Englishwoman's voice trembled.

"Yes, he is. Mr. Doston," she coaxed, "this is Heather Reed." A faint moan escaped from his white lips. "Kim, would you get him some water?" Heather requested.

Wordlessly, the young woman ran to get a glass. She returned moments later, and Heather brushed some over Doston's face and lips.

"What happened?" he murmured after a while.

"I don't know, but you're in the main barn," Heather said.

"Now, how did I . . ."

"That's what we're wondering," Kim moved closer.

"Who is she?" he asked Heather.

"Kim Rosen, Rick Spencer's fiancée," she explained.

"I remember you now," he told Kim.

"What brought you to the barn?" Heather asked.

Mr. Doston coughed as he struggled to sit up.

"He might not be up to questioning," Kim worried.

"I have to be," he muttered. "Lean me against the wall."

"Should we call an ambulance?" Heather asked.

"No," he said weakly. "Just listen. About an hour ago, I saw some people over here. I came to check things out. They were moving horses to the vet's clinic."

"How do you know?" the teenager persisted.

"Jon Kent told the blacksmith to do it. And there was a young woman with them, too," he said.

I wonder who the extra guy was that the guard mentioned? Heather asked herself.

"They took Arabian Knight and Surfer Girl to the vet's clinic," Mr. Doston went on. "I heard them say they were going to fix things."

"Oh, that's hideous!" Kim gasped.

Heather asked, "Do you know what they meant?"

The elderly man nodded. "Dr. Sandies said she was going to put down Arabian Knight so Jon could collect a wad of insurance money. She said he's worth more dead than alive."

"That's terrible!" Heather exclaimed.

"They also plan to expose Surfer Girl to a horse at the clinic who has a deadly virus. Then they'll bring her back tonight and let her spread it to Meridian, Dean Parmi's horse."

"Why?" Kim asked wide-eyed.

"I don't know," he said helplessly. "You've got to stop

them!" Mr. Doston slumped against the wall from his efforts.

"Who hurt you?" Heather asked.

"That blacksmith caught me snooping, and he knocked me out," Mr. Doston revealed. He rubbed the back of his neck.

"Kim, I'm going to the vet's," Heather announced. "You can call the police and let Mrs. Spencer know what's going on, okay?"

"Oh, Heather, you can't go there!" Kim cried. "Think of what they might do to you."

"I'm thinking of what they're going to do to those horses," Heather insisted. She paused for a moment. "I'll take Solar Wind, but I don't want to take her out on the road. Do you know a shortcut to Dr. Sandies' place, Kim?"

The young woman relented. She told Heather that the Spencer property extended all the way to the vet's clinic across the back fields.

"Pray for me," Heather called over her shoulder as she ran toward the barn where Solar Wind stayed. To her astonishment, the light was on, and the beautiful black horse was gone!

"Oh, no!" she groaned loudly. "I wonder if they took her, too!" But Heather didn't have time to find out. Instead, she moved to Master Mind's stall.

"C'mon, boy," she said, "we've got an important job ahead."

Master Mind was in no mood to cooperate, however.

He kept whinnying and tried to evade Heather's efforts to put on the bridle and saddle.

"What's the matter, Master Mind?" Heather asked, trying to calm the horse down. "Why so wound up?"

The teenager struggled with impatience when Master Mind pranced around so much that it became difficult to put on his saddle. Heather almost went for another horse, but she knew nothing about them. Fifteen minutes later, she finally mounted Master Mind. "Let's go, boy," she urged. Suddenly the horse shot out of the barn so erratically that Heather hung on for dear life. They had gone about a hundred feet when she heard sirens in the background. Although she wondered whether the police had arrived, Heather pressed forward. *I haven't got time to go back now,* she told herself.

It was a tough journey. The horse kept stopping, then bolting when Heather urged him onward. "C'mon, Master Mind," she begged, "don't act up on me, now. We've got a job to do." It was also so dark out that she had trouble seeing where she was going. Only her flashlight kept her from getting totally lost.

Suddenly, from the edge of the Spencers' property, Heather saw a black form bearing down on them like a tornado.

It's another horse! she thought wildly. Shining her flashlight on the figure, she gasped. *It's Rick Spencer, and he's riding Solar Wind!*

As Solar Wind sped toward Heather, Master Mind got spooked. He reared up and waved his front legs so wildly that Heather fell underneath him, groaning in pain. She still hurt from her other falls. But right now she was more frightened than sore. *Master Mind's going to trample me!* she thought.

16

Smooth Ride

As Heather looked up from where she lay, Master Mind eyed her malevolently. The wild look in his eyes terrified the girl. Just then Rick Spencer approached them. *I wonder what he's going to do?* she asked herself.

"Move it, Master Mind!" he commanded. "I said, 'Move it!'" When the horse kept staring Heather down, Rick took his riding crop and slapped Master Mind's flanks. The horse sprang to life, and Rick grabbed its reins, pulling it away from Heather. She watched, fascinated, as he ordered Master Mind back to the barn.

"Are you all right?" he asked, jumping off Solar Wind.

"My shoulder is sore," she said. Rick started saying something, but she interrupted him. "What are you doing here?"

"I was about to ask you the same thing," he replied.

"Why did you leave the hospital without telling him?" She still didn't trust him.

"I don't have time for that now," he said impatiently. "Some of our horses are in danger."

"Then you're going to Dr. Sandies' place to rescue them?"

"How did you know?" He was stunned.

"I've been investigating," she said.

"You!" he exclaimed, and Heather stiffened. "Listen, I don't have time for explanations. I've got to get to Dr. Sandies' place right away. You'd better go back to the barn. Mr. Doston needs help, and my mother has to be told what's going on."

"You saw Mr. Doston and didn't help him?" Heather charged.

"I called the ambulance and the police," Rick answered.

So, that's what those sirens were about, the teenager reflected. She also realized that Rick had been the fifth person mentioned by the guard. "I'm going with you. You may be too weak to handle this by yourself."

Rick sighed, but seeing her determined look, he didn't argue. Instead, Heather rode with him on Solar Wind as they took off for the veterinary clinic.

"Why was Master Mind so crazy?" she asked.

"I don't know," Rick said. "He gets spooked sometimes. I would with all those bums hanging around."

When they arrived at the vet's place less than ten minutes later, the place swarmed with police, including Captain Blake. Mrs. Blake, Tiffany, Brad, and Jenn saw Heather and ran to her.

"Oh, Heather! I was so worried about you!" Jenn hollered, hugging her friend.

"Ow!" Heather screeched.

"What did I do?" Jenn was beside herself.

"I fell off Master Mind," she said. "My shoulder hurts."

Tiffany eagerly told Heather about Katarina's e-mail letter. "We took what you had learned and added it to Katarina's message," Mrs. Blake said. "That's when we figured out the horses—and you—might be in real trouble."

At that moment, Jon Kent approached them with a scowl. Although he was in handcuffs, and an officer kept him at a safe distance, Heather still took a few steps backward.

"You little pest!" he hissed. "You ruined everything! Everything! You'll pay for this."

"That's enough!" Captain Blake ordered. "Take them away!"

One by one, police officers led Jon Kent, Cal Mahoney, Dr. Sandies, and a young woman to waiting patrol cars. The woman was wearing an oddly familiar vest. Heather suddenly realized that it was made of the same material as the scrunchie she'd found by Arabian Knight's stall!

"Are the horses all right?" she asked after the police hauled the felons away.

"Yes, thank God." Tears streamed down Tiffany's face. "Oh, Heather, we got here just in time. Dr. Sandies was getting ready to put Arabian Knight down!" She trembled from the fresh memory.

"I think it's disgusting," her mother asserted.

An hour later, Heather found herself in the lavish

living room of the Spencer estate. With her were the
Blakes, Jenn, Mr. Doston, Kim, Rick, and Mrs. Spencer.
Everyone took turns telling the story from his point of
view. Rick's was the most compelling.

"First," he said, "I want you to know I never meant to
hurt you, Kim." His blue eyes were tender as he held her
hands. "I found out about Jon's horrible scheme one
night a few weeks ago. I had felt strangely uneasy and
went to the barn to see if everything was all right. That's
when I overheard Jon and his buddy, Cal Mahoney, in
the office. They were laughing about scaring Abby
Valeet. Then they talked about their scheme. I told them
never to show their faces at my farm again. They threatened to kill me. The next day, Cal Mahoney shot me."

"How do you know it was him?" Heather shuddered.

"The night I found him in the office, Mahoney was
driving Debra Easley's red sports car. I recognized it right
before I was shot," Rick explained. "Anyway, Kim, I didn't
let you know I was leaving the hospital because I was
afraid they'd come after me again. If you had been there,
they might have killed you." He looked at her pleadingly.

Kim's eyes brimmed with tears. "I understand now."

Mrs. Spencer leaned over and kissed her son's cheek.
"I'm proud of you, Rick," she said.

He smiled shyly as Heather asked her next question.
"Rick, what were Jon and Cal doing?"

"Jon had this scheme going. He was determined to
make the Olympic team no matter what. He bought sick
horses from your friend's farm in Austria and said they

were champion material. Dr. Sandies falsified her vet reports when they arrived, so I never knew Surfer Girl, Arabian Knight, and Meridian had problems."

"That explains Surfer Girl's moodiness," Tiffany commented.

Rick nodded. "Jon's idea was eventually to put the horses down and get a huge amount of insurance money. He had taken out his own separate policy on each horse. To pay the premiums, he had embezzled money from Spencer Wood Farm. The horses were, of course, over-insured. Jon would pay his associates handsomely for making sure the horses received improper care, then pocket the difference. The night I confronted them," Rick added, "Mahoney had Arabian Knight grazing outside. Here was a horse with colic, and Mahoney was giving him grass!"

Everyone expressed revulsion that people could be so cruel to animals who trusted them.

"By undermining the horses, Jon would see that Melanie, Tiffany, and Dean wouldn't have had a chance in the Olympic trials," Rick continued. "Jon, however, had a great horse and had been training at night."

"I thought he looked tired a lot," Heather mentioned.

Rick nodded. "He was determined that nothing would stand in his way. Making the Olympic team was his obsession."

"You know the young woman they arrested?" Heather asked, thinking about the vest and the scrunchie. "How does she fit in?"

"That was Debra Easley, who's a very unhappy camper. She was in it for the money."

"I don't see why," Tiffany retorted. "Her family's loaded."

"That's part of the rub," Rick replied. "She wants to be a journalist, but her parents insist she run the farm. If Debra leaves, they'll cut off her money, and as you know, she likes the high life. This was a way for her to start on her own."

"Yeah, right in jail," Brad commented.

"What did they have her do?" Tiffany asked.

"Debra was supposed to sabotage the horses whenever she came with Cal at night. I guess she tried to undo what Brad, Abby Valeet, and the other helpers did during the day."

"Like tighten their leg bandages," Brad stated.

"Or give them moldy hay," Tiffany said.

"Or readjust hay nets," her brother added.

"That was the idea," Rick nodded.

"I found a hair scrunchie the morning Arabian Knight was really sick," Heather said, pulling the object from her backpack. "Tonight Debra was wearing the matching vest."

"I'd like to take that as evidence, if you don't mind, Heather," Captain Blake said.

The following day, the policeman shared more of the story with his family and Heather. He had discovered that Debra Easley had sent the threatening note and roses to Heather. Cal Mahoney had taken her in his blue sedan to the florist shop, since her red sports car was hidden in one of Dr. Sandies' garages.

"Mahoney also followed Kim to the pier when she met Heather there," Mr. Blake said. "Afterward, he ran you down on the bike, Heather. When Mahoney told Jon about your rendezvous at the pier, Jon started scaring Kim with nuisance phone calls."

"Remember that dog that came tearing at us a few days ago at the farm?" Jenn asked. "What was that all about?"

"Dr. Sandies arranged that," her uncle explained. "She had brought the dog with her from her clinic and ordered it to attack you."

"And those guards," Jenn added. "Were they in on the scheme?"

Her uncle shook his head. "They were only told to keep their mouths shut about what went on at night. Apparently they didn't, though."

"There's still one humongous problem," Tiffany stated a few minutes later. "Melanie, Dean, and I don't have show horses for next week's trials."

No one had an answer for that. At least not until two days later, when another e-mail message arrived from Katarina. Heather had written and told her all about the mystery. In response, Katarina informed her American friend that she was shipping to California three of her family's top show horses.

"They are on loan from us to help make up for the problems you have suffered because of our trainer's corrupt ways," she had written. "Please forgive our farm, and have your riders do their best in the ten-day trials."

Tiffany was thrilled with the news. She eagerly told Melanie and Dean at the farm that day. "This is an answer to my prayers," Tiffany smiled.

Melanie looked apologetic. "Tiffany, I'm sorry for the things I said to you. I behaved badly."

"I accept," Tiffany said graciously. She waited for Dean to say something similar as Heather, Jenn, and Brad watched.

"I still intend to beat you both," he remarked pompously.

"Some things never change," Brad shook his head in disgust.

"Like Heather's ability to solve a mystery," Jenn grinned.

"Or that I'm already looking for another case," the teenage detective sighed.